Pippa Parker

Past
TENSe

Liz Hedgecock

WHITE
RHINO
BOOKS

Copyright © Liz Hedgecock, 2020

All rights reserved. Apart from any use permitted under UK copyright law, no part of this publication may be reproduced, stored in a retrieval system, or transmitted, in any form or by any means, electronic, mechanical, photocopying, recording or otherwise, without the prior written permission of the copyright owner.

This is a work of fiction. Names, characters, businesses, places, events and incidents are either the products of the author's imagination or used in a fictitious manner. Any resemblance to actual persons, living or dead, or actual events is purely coincidental.

ISBN-13: 979-8656594394

For Stephen,
who wouldn't start on the wine without me

Chapter 1

Pippa Parker eyed the stroller folded up in the porch. It looked as if it was biding its time, itching to give her a cut or a trapped finger when she unfolded it. *I should put it away*, she thought. *Or sell it on. Ruby doesn't use it any more.* She touched the durable red fabric which she had sponged clean of mud and worse so many times. *It needs a good clean first. But now is not the time.* After a busy afternoon of work, it was time to pick up Ruby, fetch Freddie from school, and spend quality time with the children.

She considered taking the car, for speed, then shook her head. *It's a beautiful spring day*, she told herself. *You ought to get some exercise; you've been slaving over a hot laptop for two hours.* Pippa laced up her trainers, picked up her keys, decided that despite the bright sun she would still wear a jacket, and pulled the door shut behind her.

The walk to Sheila's house gave Pippa time to clear her head of the various things buzzing around it. While Serendipity, her crafty friend, had taken on a manager for

1

her growing business at Pippa's recommendation, Pippa was still acting as a virtual PA, managing Serendipity's bookings and fielding the more outlandish enquiries. And on the subject of outlandishness, she was still working with Lady Higginbotham. Quite apart from the Summer Proms, which were becoming a regular feature in Much Gadding's calendar, Pippa had the holiday lets to manage, and also an increasing amount of wedding bookings. And with spring in the air, enquiries were increasing at an alarming rate. *'Tis the season*, thought Pippa, as she marched along.

And then there was Jeff.

Pippa had been rather surprised when Lila buttonholed her at the school gate the previous morning. 'Can I have a word?' she muttered.

'Of course,' said Pippa. 'What's it about?'

'I was wondering,' said Lila, 'if you had space for another client. For event stuff.'

'What sort of client?'

Lila looked elaborately around her. 'Do you have time for a coffee?'

'A quick one, yes,' said Pippa, wondering if Lila had the ear of some famous person, and somehow had never mentioned it.

Lila chatted about this and that until they were sitting at her breakfast bar with mugs of milky coffee. 'So come on,' said Pippa. 'Who's this mystery client?'

Lila bit her lip. 'It's Jeff.'

'Jeff?' Pippa stared at her. 'But *you're* managing Jeff and the group.'

'I am,' said Lila. 'Well, sort of. The thing is…' She sipped her coffee, then set the mug down. 'There's a bit of a conflict of interest.'

'Um, in what way?' If anything, Pippa had thought Lila was almost more keen for Short Back And Sides to succeed than Jeff was.

Lila grimaced. 'It isn't that I don't want him to succeed. It's just—' She attempted to run a hand through her curls, but it got stuck part-way through. 'They're doing really well,' she said, untangling it.

'But that's good, isn't it?' said Pippa.

'Yes! And he's really pleased.' She chewed her lower lip.

'I'm sorry, but I don't understand.' Pippa tried not to stare at her friend. 'What are you trying to say?'

'I want us to try for a baby,' Lila said, in a rush. 'I don't want him to be doing gigs all the time, or even, maybe, on a tour.' Suddenly she looked guilty. 'An email landed in the Short Back and Sides inbox two days ago. It was the manager from Rumours in Gadcester.'

Pippa grinned. 'Gadcester's premier nightspot bar none?'

'That's the one,' said Lila miserably. 'He wants to know if Short Back and Sides would be available for a trial spot on a Wednesday, with a view to a residency if it works out.'

'And what did you say?'

Lila studied the worktop. 'I didn't,' she said. 'I haven't answered the email yet. And that's why I'm asking if you'll take Jeff on. I'm not the best person to do it any more. I don't want to hold him back, or the group, but…' She rubbed her nose, still not meeting Pippa's eyes.

'Of course I shall,' said Pippa. 'Although I think you should talk to Jeff.' Lila gazed up at Pippa. 'He does know about the baby thing, doesn't he?'

'Yes,' said Lila. 'At least, he ought to.'

'So you haven't said it in so many words?'

'I've dropped plenty of hints,' said Lila. 'I mean, surely there's only so many times I can wander into Baby Gap with him before he gets it.'

Pippa sighed. 'Lila, you know it doesn't work like that. You do actually have to tell him straight out that you would like to try for a baby.'

Lila's grip on her mug tightened. 'He ought to know! I mean, I'm thirty-three, there isn't much time left! And Bella's five now. If I don't get a move on there will be a huge gap…'

'OK.' Pippa put a hand on Lila's arm. 'I can put Ruby into Little Puffins for an extra half day, and take Jeff on as a client, if that's what you want. But there are two conditions.'

Lila looked very worried. 'What are they?'

Pippa smiled. 'One, you have to tell him about the baby thing. I mean properly. And the other one is that you don't stick your nose in. Jeff's sensible. He's not going to get carried away and go off on some massive tour of medium-size venues in the Home Counties.'

Lila giggled. 'When you put it like that…'

'Exactly,' said Pippa. 'I suggest we try it for three months and see how it goes. Then if it doesn't work out, you can have him back.' She finished her coffee. 'Better?'

'Better.' Lila managed a shaky smile. 'Thanks, Pippa.'

'No problem,' said Pippa. 'Let me know when you've told him.'

Lila ran her hands through her hair. 'Oh heck, now I'll have to think of a reason.'

'Just tell him you think he needs a professional,' said Pippa. 'I'm not sure I'm a professional, but he'll like that explanation.'

***

Pippa came to and found herself ringing Sheila's doorbell. She took her finger off it abruptly, uncertain exactly how long she had been pressing it for. As she did so, the door opened. 'I am coming, you know,' said Sheila, quite mildly, considering.

'Sorry,' said Pippa. 'I was daydreaming. Has Ruby been OK?'

'Yes, she has,' said Sheila without hesitation.

'Really?' said Pippa.

'Yes, really.' She laughed. 'We were doing crafts. There was a page in the supermarket magazine about making an Easter egg box, so that's what we've been doing. She's finishing it off now.'

'Oh,' said Pippa, envisaging her daughter covered in paint, glue, and heaven knows what else.

'Come in and have a look,' said Sheila. 'I helped a bit, but she's done ever so well.'

Pippa walked into Sheila's dining room. The table was covered with newspaper and Ruby, wearing one of Sheila's aprons, was sitting, paintbrush in hand, frowning at an egg box. On the lid of the box was painted most of an Easter chick. 'Can you do feet, Nana?' asked Ruby. 'Hello, Mummy! I did a box!'

'So you did,' said Pippa. 'It's very good.' And it was surprisingly good. The chick, while slightly Picassoish in feature, was recognisable as such, and around it were stuck multicoloured hearts and diamonds in a regular pattern.

'Can I take it home?' asked Ruby.

'I'd say yes,' said Pippa, 'but it needs to dry first. We don't want to smudge your chick.'

'No,' said Ruby. 'That would be a disaaaaaahster.' Once again Pippa wondered where her daughter got her words from, and drew a blank.

'I'll keep it till next time,' said Sheila. 'Hadn't you better go and get Freddie?'

'Oh gosh, yes,' said Pippa. 'I swear time runs away with me.'

'Wait until you're my age,' said Sheila. 'I swear someone messes with the clock when I'm not looking.'

They said their goodbyes, and set off for the primary school. Ruby trotted beside Pippa, a slightly damp little hand in hers. *Far too grown-up for a stroller*, thought Pippa. *I'll give it a clean at the weekend, and put it on eBay, or the village Facebook group.*

'When is Easter?' asked Ruby suddenly.

'I'm not sure,' said Pippa. 'It changes every year.'

'Why?' Ruby looked up at her as she stumped along.

'Um, I don't know. Something to do with the moon?'

'Oh,' said Ruby. 'Google it, Mummy.'

'Yes I could, couldn't I?' said Pippa. 'Thank you for

your suggestion.'

The increasing babble of little voices told Pippa that they were nearly at the school. The playground was full already. She checked her watch: one minute to go.

The bell rang, and the playground held its breath, waiting for the first door to open. There was Freddie, galloping out with his classmates. Pippa narrowed her eyes. Was he taller than Henry now? And he towered over Bella.

Lila sidled up. 'I told Jeff,' she volunteered.

'About the – you know?'

'I'm working up to that,' said Lila. 'I did the professional thing, like you said, and he agreed.' She fumbled in a pocket, and handed Pippa a folded piece of paper. 'That's the email address and password for Short Back and Sides. I'll send an email with everything else. So it's ready when you are.'

'Right,' said Pippa. 'Thanks.'

'Pleasure doing business with you,' said Lila, and grinned. 'Come on Bella, home time!' She bounced off, looking considerably happier.

Pippa glanced at the piece of paper, then stuffed it in her pocket. Freddie was chasing Dylan round the playground, weaving between little knots of parents and children. She sighed. 'Freddie, stop that.'

Freddie stopped dead, then back-pedalled. 'I was exercising, Mummy.'

'We'll go by the village green on the way home, and you can exercise on that,' said Pippa.

'Will the ice cream van be there?' asked Freddie,

suddenly very interested indeed.

'Possibly,' admitted Pippa.

'Let's go!' Freddie grabbed Ruby's hand and whirled her around. 'Ice cream! Ice cream!'

'Only possibly,' warned Pippa. 'Come along, you two.'

As it turned out the ice cream van was at the green, and Pippa allowed them a Mini Milk each. Afterwards the children played tag according to complicated rules that, according to Freddie, were the school norm, but somehow always resulted in Ruby's tag not counting.

Pippa sat on a bench and watched them. *They're growing up*, she thought. *Maybe it is time for new things.* She eased Lila's piece of paper from her pocket. A new client. An interesting new client with a lot of potential. So long as she didn't wind Lila up by letting Jeff get too famous. *I'll deal with that when it comes*, she thought, smiling. *But at least it will keep my mind off – everything else.* She looked at her watch. *Time for SuperMouse soon*, she thought, then told herself off for living by the schedule of her kids' favourite TV show.

Chapter 2

'Come on, Ruby,' said Pippa. 'Let's cross the road.'

She began to step out but Ruby tugged hard on her hand. 'No, Mummy! There's a van!'

'It's a long way away,' said Pippa. 'Come along.'

'It could kill us,' said Ruby.

'I doubt it,' said Pippa. But now the van was too close to cross.

'See,' said Ruby. 'Really big.'

The van rumbled past. *Logan Removals*, it said on the side. *Trusted throughout Gadcestershire*.

Pippa blinked. *That could be—*

'We can cross,' said Ruby. 'Why aren't we crossing?'

'OK, OK,' said Pippa, and walked Ruby across the empty road.

That was probably Jim's van. Not that it matters.

She had heard about it one afternoon, through a text from Mandy. *All change at the police station. I'm afraid you'll have to put up with Gabe Gannet.*

Pippa had a distinct sinking feeling. *What have I done*

to deserve that? she replied.

Inspector F wants to give Gabe more experience of community policing, so he's coming to you.

Pippa's fingers itched to type: *What about Jim?* She sat on her hands for two minutes. Eventually, teeth gritted, she typed: *I see.*

And he wants Jim to work more closely with him at HQ. I'll have to put up with Jim's rubbish coffee at work too now.

Every silver lining has a cloud, Pippa texted back. Then she turned her phone over, and went to make a strong cup of tea.

It doesn't matter, she told herself as the kettle boiled. *Nothing was ever going to happen. Nothing ought to happen. It would be a terrible idea.*

The kettle pinged, and she drowned her teabag.

'It's just that he's a very good local policeman,' she said, getting a spoon and squeezing the teabag against the side of the cup. 'I know PC Gannet has to learn the ropes, but I wish he didn't have to do it here.' She scooped the teabag out of the cup, flicked it at the bin, and was savagely pleased when it went in. Then she got the milk, and discovered that the teabag had split and specks of leaf were floating on the surface of her tea. *Like dead bodies*, she thought, and rummaged for the tea strainer.

Pippa had waited for a communication from Jim. When it wasn't forthcoming, she had, in a bad mood, texted him. *So I hear you're off to Gadcester.*

A reply had come ten minutes later. *Yes, that's right.*

What do I say? Pippa thought. *Congratulations? We'll*

miss you? I'll miss you?

Her phone buzzed again a few minutes later. *I'll miss Much Gadding, but it's time for new things.*

Pippa picked up her phone. *Yes, I suppose it is. Well done.*

And that was where they had left it. She and Mandy texted more often now, anyway. It was Mandy who told her that they'd decided to get a flat in Gadcester. *We're renting, and it makes no sense for us both to drive there and back every day.*

No, it doesn't, Pippa replied. *You'll have to come over for dinner some time.* But she suspected that would never happen.

'Mummy!'

Pippa looked down at Ruby, who was pulling on her sleeve again. Then she realised they had reached the nursery. 'Sorry, Ruby, I was miles away.'

'No, Mummy. You're here. Silly Mummy,' said Ruby.

Alicia greeted her at the nursery door. 'We wondered if you were coming, Ruby,' she said. 'Don't you usually drop off before school?'

'Yes,' said Pippa. 'Could I have a word?'

'I'll talk to Mrs Snell,' said Alicia, doubtfully. She disappeared, but returned wearing a beaming smile. 'Come this way.'

It was Pippa's first time in Mrs Snell's office. Really, it was more of a cupboard than an office; instead of certificates or pictures, the walls were lined with shelves full of nappies, wipes, and other paraphernalia.

Mrs Snell herself was tucked into a corner, behind the

laptop. 'What can I do for you, Mrs Parker?' she asked, taking her glasses off. 'I'm glad you popped in, because I want to talk to you, too.'

'Talk to me?' Pippa felt non-specific guilt wash over her. *Ruby hasn't done something, has she?*

Mrs Snell smiled. 'Ruby's doing fine. In fact, that's why I wanted to talk to you. When was her birthday? She's October, isn't she?'

'That's right, yes,' said Pippa. 'October the twenty-fifth.'

'Thought so,' said Mrs Snell. 'I was wondering what you thought about moving her into the Cygnet Room. I think she's ready.'

'Already?' Pippa goggled.

'I'd say so,' said Mrs Snell. 'She's two and a half, and her record shows that she has all the skills to manage pretty well in the Cygnet Room. Plus I must admit that it would help us. We have room for one more child in Cygnets, you see, and then we can move another child into Ducklings.'

'I see,' said Pippa. *Ruby, a preschooler!*

'You look a bit surprised.'

'I am,' said Pippa, slowly. 'I still think of her as my baby a lot of the time.'

'Oh, she'll always be that,' said Mrs Snell, comfortably. 'My baby is twenty-six now, you know.'

'Oh don't,' said Pippa.

'But you don't have any particular objections, Mrs Parker?' asked Mrs Snell. 'Anyway, I'm forgetting my manners. What was it you wanted to see me about?'

'Oh,' said Pippa. 'I wondered if I could book Ruby in for an extra half-day a week. I've got some extra work, you see. I don't mind when,' she added hastily.

'Let me see.' Mrs Snell stared at her laptop screen. 'It depends how full we are, and we are quite full at the moment.'

Pippa crossed her fingers under the desk.

'Mmm,' said Mrs Snell. 'I have good news and bad news. I have got room on Wednesday afternoons, but only in the Cygnet Room. It's the staffing ratios, you see.'

'Then I suppose that settles it,' said Pippa.

'Excellent,' said Mrs Snell. 'I'll recalculate your bill, and send you an email. When would you like the new arrangement to start?'

'Um, next week?'

'Wonderful,' said Mrs Snell. 'I'll have a printout ready for you when you pick Ruby up later.'

Pippa thanked her and left, wondering how it was that with Mrs Snell, she always felt as if she'd been completely outmanoeuvred. Perhaps it was because she spent most of the day getting strong-willed children to do things they'd really rather not.

Off to work, Pippa, she told herself. *These events won't run themselves.* She gave Ruby another kiss for good measure and walked briskly home, trying to muster up energy for the task before her.

***

Pippa made a cup of tea, took it into the dining room, and opened up her laptop. *Here goes*, she thought. First she would check her own email, then see if she could get into the Short Back and Sides inbox. *Come on*, she urged the spinning rainbow circle.

Eventually, her email inbox opened up. At the top was a message titled *Invitation*. It was marked urgent, and was from someone called Jeremy Lightfoot.

'Jeremy Lightfoot,' murmured Pippa. 'How do I know that name?' She shrugged and opened the email.

Dear Mrs Parker,

Apologies for springing into your inbox unannounced. You may not have heard of me, but I am a professor at George Hudson University in York, and you may possibly have seen me on television, since I occasionally present documentaries for the BBC.

Gosh, thought Pippa.

I am writing to invite you to a meeting at Much Gadding church hall on Tuesday 19th March, at 7 o'clock.

The purpose of the meeting is to discuss the possibility of staging a small event this summer to mark the 19oth anniversary of the birth of Clementina Stoate. I'm sure you know the name; she was an acclaimed poet who resided in the village, and whose cottage is still standing.

I have it on good authority that you are a mainstay of village events, and I would like to gauge your opinion on what we can do.

Further, this event is not an end in itself. Obviously the bicentenary of Clementina Stoate's birth will take place in 2029, and I would view the event this summer as a sort of run-up to gauge interest. I shall be doing my best to whip up a Stoate frenzy in academic and arts circles, and any help in achieving this would be very much welcomed.

I look forward to meeting you on the 19th.
Yours sincerely,
Jeremy Lightfoot

Beneath the email was a set of web links. The first pointed to a BBC webpage for a documentary on someone Pippa had never heard of, while the following ones linked to Jeremy Lightfoot's books.

'I'm not sure he needs my help,' murmured Pippa. She sipped her tea and thought. *Well, I said I wanted new things, and now I have them.* On impulse she found Clementina Stoate on Wikipedia. The entry just about reached the bottom of her screen: a Victorian poet who had lived quietly in the countryside, become briefly famous, then ceased to write after the death of her husband.

'I'm really not sure what you're going to make of that, Jeremy,' said Pippa, 'but you're welcome to try.' She imagined a Victorian fayre, with the residents of Much Gadding resplendent in top hats and crinolines. *Perhaps both together.* She giggled, reread the email, then wrote a short reply accepting the invitation and put the event in her calendar. *I'd better read some of her poetry before then,* she thought. *If I can get hold of any.*

Pippa scanned the rest of her inbox. Two replies from bands she wanted to book for the Summer Proms – very good – and a quote from her marquee supplier. She opened it, and winced. Clearly the growing profile of the Proms was encouraging people to bump up their prices. *I'll see about that*, she thought, and wrote herself a note to get three more quotes to see if she could find a better offer.

Now for Short Back and Sides, she thought, taking a deep draught of tea in preparation. She fished Lila's piece of paper out of the pocket of her laptop case, and typed in the username and password. *Should I change it?* she thought, then dismissed the idea. For all she knew, Jeff checked it regularly. Although Lila hadn't given that impression…

Pippa groaned as the inbox opened. 590 emails, with 190 unopened, and no filing system. *Oh, Lila…* Pippa went to make a fresh cup of tea and got herself a biscuit as an anticipatory reward for tackling whatever horror she was about to find.

First things first, she thought, and looked for the email from Rumours. It wasn't far from the top, and the subject line was *Great Opportunity!!!* Pippa shuddered, and opened it. The email was written in an aggressive, jagged font.

Dear Short Back and Sides!

Jed James here from Rumours, Gadcester's premier nightspot bar none.

We're after dynamic new acts to spice up our midweek offering, and I'm giving you the chance to strut your stuff on a Wednesday of your choice. If it goes well, maybe I could make you a permanent fixture.

Drop me a line, and let's get talking.

Must dash,
Jed

Pippa giggled, and texted Jeff. *Would you and SB&S like to do a gig at Rumours on a Wednesday sometime? There's an invite in your email.*

Her phone buzzed five minutes later. *Sorry for delayed reply, just dealing with a customer. Yes please definitely, Jeff. PS Thanks*

Pippa smiled. If that was Jeff's idea of a delayed reply, he would probably be her easiest client. Lady Higginbotham was either all over everything like a rash, or impossibly indecisive. Serendipity was a dream when you could get hold of her, which was becoming increasingly difficult these days. Her manager was nice, but frighteningly efficient. Which, Pippa supposed, was exactly how she ought to be. *I should probably take a leaf out of her book*, she thought, feeling inadequate. *Anyway.* She hit *Reply*.

Dear Mr James,

I have just spoken to Short Back and Sides, and they are delighted to accept your kind offer.

Please could you let me know possible dates, and I'll sort something out.

Yours sincerely,
Pippa Parker

She pressed *Send*, waited for the whoosh, then created a new folder named *Bookings* and moved the original email into it. *There*, she thought. *It's a start, at least.*

One down, 589 to go.

Pippa sighed, and bit into her biscuit. It was going to be a long morning.

Chapter 3

'Do I look all right?' asked Pippa, scrutinising herself in the mirror.

Simon regarded her critically. 'You look fine. But I'm not sure how you're supposed to look when you're meeting an academic. Shouldn't you be in a tweed jacket and a bow tie?'

'Shall I add a pipe while I'm at it?' Pippa had rejected her usual jeans in favour of a pair of black trousers, and an actual blouse with buttons in place of a T-shirt. 'It probably doesn't matter what I wear, anyway. I get the impression that I'm there to do the heavy lifting.'

'I hope you don't mean that literally,' said Simon.

'Well, I don't know who else is going to be there.'

Simon raised an eyebrow. 'You mean you didn't use your super detective skills to find out?'

'I've been too busy,' said Pippa.

And she had, since it had taken her some time to track down any of Clementina Stoate's poetry.

Her first stop had been the library. 'Got any poetry?'

she asked Norm.

Norm lowered his newspaper. 'That's rather a departure from your usual fare, Pippa.'

'I know,' said Pippa. 'I'm looking for poetry by Clementina Stoate. Our local poet.'

'Indeed,' said Norm. 'We haven't any, because it's out.'

'Is it now,' said Pippa. 'Could I ask who borrowed it?'

'You could,' said Norm, tapping his ledger. 'But I'm afraid I couldn't tell you. People's choice of reading matter is between me and this ledger.'

Pippa sighed. 'All right then, can you tell me when it will be back in?'

Norm considered. 'I don't think that's classified information.' He opened the ledger and consulted it. Pippa noted that he didn't need to turn back any pages. The borrow must be recent. 'Two weeks from yesterday.'

'Oh,' said Pippa. 'That's a bit late for me.'

'Mmm,' said Norm. 'Even if it weren't, you'd have to go on the waiting list. Clementina Stoate is hot property.'

'Oh well,' said Pippa, 'back to the golden age of crime, I guess. You haven't had a run on that, have you?'

Norm smiled. 'Only from you.'

In the end Pippa had tracked down a few poems in an internet poetry archive. Project Gutenberg didn't appear to have digitised her work. *And that's saying something*, thought Pippa. She read the five poems and came away not much the wiser. One was dull, three were enjoyable nature-based poems, and the last one was downright confusing. *I have no idea what that's about*, she thought, when she finished it. *That probably means it's very good and important*. She printed off the poems, just in case, and put them in a plastic wallet. One never knew what might come in handy.

And now it was ten to seven and she ought to be heading to the meeting. 'I'd better go,' she said, fiddling with an earring. 'Are you sure you can manage bedtime?'

'Pippa,' said Simon, 'the children have been fed, they're in their pyjamas, and all I have to do is make sure their teeth are clean, tuck them up and read a story. I'm not completely incapable.'

Pippa smiled. 'Course not.'

'Then off you go,' said Simon. 'Enjoy your evening with Jeremy Lightfoot. Who knows, maybe you'll have a starring role in his next documentary.'

'I seriously doubt it,' said Pippa, and went downstairs.

It was one of those spring evenings which are bright but surprisingly cool, and Pippa was glad of the cardigan she had caught up at the last minute. The church hall tended to be draughty at the best of times, and she had no idea how long she would be sitting listening to people drone on. *Not that it will necessarily be boring*, she told herself, *but, you know.*

She arrived at the hall bang on seven o'clock, and found the door ajar. People were already sitting round a horseshoe of trestle tables, the ends pointing towards the back of the hall. A separate small table had been set up in the centre, on which was a projector and laptop. And fiddling with the projector was a tall lean man wearing a cream linen jacket and coral-coloured trousers. *Jeremy Lightfoot, I presume*, thought Pippa.

She tried to slip in unobtrusively, but a strident voice said, 'Hello, Pippa,' and she came eye to eye with Marge. 'There's a seat here.'

'Oh yes, thanks,' said Pippa, sliding into it.

Jeremy Lightfoot fixed a beady eye on her. 'And you would be?' he enquired.

'Pippa Parker,' said Pippa. 'You sent me an invite.'

'Pippa Parker, Pippa Parker...' Jeremy Lightfoot gazed at the ceiling as if his list of participants might be there. 'Oh yes, so I did.' His slightly querulous expression was replaced by a smile which Pippa felt sure he thought of as his charming smile. 'So glad you could make it. We have a few . . . extras, but I'm sure all will be well.' His gaze slid sideways to Marge, and the charming smile disappeared rapidly. 'We're waiting for one more person, and then we can begin.'

'Am I late?' said a timid voice at the door, and Pippa found herself looking at Lady Higginbotham.

Jeremy Lightfoot's face lit up. 'No, no, Lady Higginbotham, you are absolutely on time. And we would never have started without you, in any case.'

A snort came from Pippa's left. Jeremy Lightfoot sprang into action, fetching an extra chair, frowning at people to move up, and placing it elaborately for Lady Higginbotham, who murmured her thanks then made herself as small as possible.

Jeremy Lightfoot closed the door with a flourish and returned to centre stage. 'Thank you for coming, everybody,' he declared, in a carrying voice. 'I'm sorry for such short notice, but I happened to be filming nearby, so it seemed an excellent opportunity to drop in. I am in the course of filming a documentary...'

Pippa looked around the table. Lady Higginbotham was there, and Norm, and Malcolm Allison from the Much Gadding Archaeological Society, and Marge, and on Marge's other side, a small elderly woman whom she didn't recognise. *I wonder who she is*, she thought. And why has Marge got herself in here? *I wouldn't have thought this was her sort of thing at all.*

'So to bring us up to speed, I thought it would be useful to give you a short overview of Clementina Stoate and her work.' Jeremy Lightfoot went to the laptop, brought up a video, and pressed *Play*.

What followed was a PowerPoint presentation narrated by Jeremy, giving the basic facts of Clementina Stoate's life and work, with floaty classical music as a backing soundtrack. Pippa felt herself drifting off, and stared hard at the back wall of the hall.

'So as you see, Clementina Stoate has been shamefully neglected,' said Jeremy Lightfoot. 'I maintain that she is, in fact, one of the major female poets of the nineteenth century, despite her comparatively small output, and she ought to have a much higher profile than she currently does.' He surveyed the table with a slightly wolfish smile. 'And that is where we come in.'

Do we, thought Pippa.

'It is incredibly important that the house where Clementina Stoate lived, and wrote most of her poetry, is still standing. And thanks to the conservation order in Much Gadding, it retains many of the original features from Mrs Stoate's time. I would maintain that this ought to be open to the public as a site of national interest.' His eyes fell on the woman Pippa didn't know.

She jumped as if someone had pricked her with a pin. 'Oh, but I don't know about that. I mean, it isn't a large house.'

'Well no, of course not,' said Jeremy Lightfoot indulgently. 'But it's absolutely vital to Victorian scholars to be able to see the place where Clementina Stoate wrote her poems. Surely you would agree that it is an important heritage site, Daphne.'

Daphne murmured something, and stared at the table. Pippa felt sure that if she could have, she would have rolled into a ball.

'The thing is, Jeremy,' said Marge, 'Clementina Stoate's former home is Daphne's actual home, and she doesn't necessarily want to open it up to every Tom, Dick and Harry.'

'And I never said she should,' said Jeremy Lightfoot. 'But I maintain that we could do more.'

'Oh, we could always do more,' said Marge, looking disgusted.

Jeremy Lightfoot appeared distinctly ruffled, and Pippa decided to step in before he and Marge came to blows. 'You mentioned an event in the summer, Mr Lightfoot,' she said. 'Could you tell us a little more about what you have in mind?'

Jeremy Lightfoot beamed. 'I'd be delighted,' he said. 'I was thinking of a small literary festival to be held in the village. A sort of celebration. We could, I am sure, present actors reading a selection of poems, and hold talks by leading academics on how Mrs Stoate's poetry fits in with other, perhaps more well-known, works from the period. Of course there will also be opportunities to provide Victorian food and drink to members of the public who, perhaps, would be more interested in that than the literary element.'

If he puffs up any more he'll explode, thought Pippa. 'And I presume you're looking for someone to organise that,' she said.

Jeremy Lightfoot's smile never wavered. 'Oh yes,' he said. 'The difficulty is, you see, that with my university teaching and my other commitments, I cannot be as hands-on as I would like. For example, there would be volunteers to organise, bookings to make, television and newspaper opportunities to coordinate... I mean, just managing admissions to the house would probably take up one person's time.'

'Admissions to the house?' quavered Daphne. 'You never said—'

'But of course people will want to see the house!' exclaimed Mr Lightfoot. 'That will be the highlight of the whole thing!'

Daphne looked ready to faint.

'If it's allowed,' said Marge firmly.

'And how are we going to afford this?' asked Pippa. 'What do you propose to charge people?'

'Oh no, we won't charge them,' said Jeremy Lightfoot. 'Culture ought to be free. No, my intention is that we would apply for funding. I am sure that the Arts Council would be interested in supporting such a prestigious event. Not to mention your local council, whichever that is, and I daresay local businesses would wish to sponsor it too.'

'So you need somebody to drum up support as well,' said Pippa.

'I am sure the local university would also like to be involved,' said Jeremy. 'Perhaps some of the students will be interested in volunteering, for example. It would be excellent experience for them. So, what does everyone think?' He gazed around the table. 'A wonderful summer festival, celebrating an important and neglected local author.'

Norm raised a hand. 'I must admit that, apart from the plaque, I'd never heard of Clementina Stoate until I received your email.'

'This is exactly why we must make the most of this opportunity!' Jeremy's expression became roguish, and Pippa realised he was looking at Lady Higginbotham. 'Lady Higginbotham, I'm sure *you* had heard of Clementina Stoate.'

'Oh yes,' said Lady Higginbotham, as if she did not want to be questioned further.

'I knew you would have,' said Jeremy Lightfoot. 'Could I perhaps prevail on you to consider hosting the festival at the hall? It would be a beautiful setting, and of course everyone will be very well-behaved.'

Pippa imagined a bevy of students letting off steam on Lady Higginbotham's lawn after a long weekend of volunteering. But Lady Higginbotham wore the abstracted expression of someone working out a complicated sum.

Pippa suspected she was; subtracting the cost of the event, and the trouble it might cause, from the increased bookings which would follow the debut of Higginbotham Hall on local and even national television.

'I don't see why not,' she said, smiling at Jeremy. 'And of course people will help.'

'Wonderful!' Jeremy Lightfoot's face lit up. He loped round the table and gave Lady Higginbotham a gentle squeeze. 'We are up and running!'

Lady Higginbotham giggled like a schoolgirl. *This will be very difficult to manage*, thought Pippa, with a sigh.

'If we are going to stage this event,' she said, 'we need to have regular meetings to discuss the scope of it, who does what, and what funding to apply for. And we should sell tickets. Local people are perfectly used to the idea that events don't come for free.'

Jeremy Lightfoot gave her a reproving look. 'Well, no,' he said. 'But I don't like the idea of restricting admission.'

Marge snorted again. 'You want to stage a festival about a poet even the locals haven't heard of. Frankly, Jeremy, you'll be lucky to get twenty people.'

'Oh, I'm not just thinking local,' said Jeremy Lightfoot. 'This will be national. International, even.' He spread his hands wide. 'Not yet, obviously. But if we can make a success of a small event this summer, then for Clementina's bicentenary in 2029 we could do something much bigger. Possibly coinciding with the launch of an edition of collected poems and letters.' His gaze rested on Daphne. 'I'm sure you must have some of your ancestor's papers tucked away.'

'Only a few letters,' said Daphne.

Jeremy came closer. 'How many?'

Daphne looked as if she wanted the ground to swallow her up. 'Maybe fifty,' she said.

'*Fifty?*' Jeremy's eyes almost popped out of their sockets. 'But none of the academic journals mention more than twelve!'

'It's private correspondence,' Daphne whispered, her voice dry as paper.

'Good heavens.' Jeremy Lightfoot put his hand on his heart. 'What a discovery,' he breathed. 'I need to sit down.' He pulled out a chair and sank into it, staring at the wall, which still showed the projected image of a tall stout lady in black. Eventually, he turned to Daphne. 'May I – may I see them?'

Daphne's hands twisted. 'I—'

'We could go now,' said Jeremy. 'We've done all we reasonably can here tonight, and I have an hour before my train.'

Marge put a hand on Daphne's shoulder. 'You don't have to agree to anything,' she said. 'He can always come back.'

'Oh, but it isn't as easy as that,' said Jeremy Lightfoot. 'I am very busy, you know. And seeing the letters, the actual letters—'

'I'm coming with you,' said Marge, grimly.

'Could I see them too, perhaps?' asked Lady Higginbotham. 'To help me – understand her a little more.'

'In that case,' said Pippa, 'why don't we all go, and get it over with?'

'Good idea,' said Marge. 'There isn't much.' She laughed. 'You can see what there is to see in about ten minutes.'

Daphne looked rather hurt, then smiled bravely.

'Come on, then,' said Marge, getting up with a great scraping of her chair. 'Let's get this done. We wouldn't want Mr Lightfoot to miss his train, now would we?' She gave Jeremy Lightfoot a distinctly venomous glare which had no effect whatsoever.

Jeremy bounced out of his chair and began to pack away his equipment. 'Five minutes, Daphne, and I'm all yours.'

Daphne's eyes opened very wide, and she shuddered.

Jeremy Lightfoot zipped his laptop into the bag, slung it over his shoulder, and grinned. 'Let's go! Lead the way, Daphne.' He urged Daphne forward with a grand sweep of his arm, and the rest of the party straggled in her hesitant wake.

Chapter 4

Jeremy Lightfoot buttonholed Lady Higginbotham almost immediately. 'Would you like an arm?' he asked, offering his.

Lady Higginbotham blushed, and took it. *She's really under his spell*, thought Pippa. Then she felt a prod in her ribs. Suppressing an exclamation, she found Marge next to her. 'Drop back a bit,' Marge muttered.

Frowning at her, Pippa did as she was told, until they were perhaps ten feet behind Norm, who sauntered along with his hands in his pockets, whistling as if he always visited a Victorian poet's cottage at this time of the evening. 'What is it?' she asked.

'I want you to refuse to have anything to do with this malarkey,' said Marge. 'Poor Daphne will have a heart attack.'

Pippa considered her response. On one hand, what Jeremy Lightfoot was proposing sounded like an awful lot of work. However, she had said she was interested in trying new things, and perhaps this was one of the new things she should try. After all, Jeremy Lightfoot seemed very good at persuading the right people. 'How did you get into the meeting?' she asked. 'I take it Jeremy didn't invite you.'

'No, he did not,' said Marge, stomping beside her. 'Daphne asked me to come.'

'Oh yes, how do you know each other?' Pippa couldn't imagine bluff, abrasive Marge and timid Daphne getting on.

'School friends,' said Marge. 'Well, we weren't really friends at school, but when people start moving away, and then dying, you sort of stick to who's left.' She fell silent for a moment as they walked along. 'If he could, that man wouldn't have invited Daphne either. He'd have come up with his plans, got funding, then presented it as a fait accompli.'

'I don't think that's possible,' said Pippa.

'Hopefully not,' said Marge. 'I just don't want Daphne to be worried. She isn't very strong.'

'I can see that,' said Pippa. If anything, Daphne was moving more slowly the closer they got to her house. Or Clementina Stoate's house, as she was already starting to think of it. 'Isn't she proud of her – is it her famous ancestor?'

'Great great something aunt,' said Marge. 'And no, not particularly. When we were kids they made us do her poems at school, and the kids never let Daphne forget it. She was always called Daphne's boring auntie.' She sniggered. 'Daphne wanted to leave the village and Clementina Stoate behind, but she never could. Poorly mother, you see, and when that was all over, she felt it was too late.'

'Oh,' said Pippa. She looked ahead at the small, bowed, creeping figure of Daphne. 'If there isn't much to see, maybe we can persuade Jeremy Lightfoot to concentrate his energies on putting on a big show at Higginbotham Hall.'

'True,' conceded Marge.

They had, at last, reached the row of cottages which bore the blue plaque. They gathered outside, and watched Daphne rummage in her bag. Eventually she brought out some keys, with a plastic keyring of Gadcester Cathedral attached. 'They always go straight to the bottom,' she apologised.

'Of course they do,' said Jeremy Lightfoot, grinning.

Pippa stepped back for a moment to look at the house. It was quaint, timbered, with small-paned, slightly wonky windows. Three steps led up to the door, which was a stout wooden one, painted black, with a well-polished brass knocker. The curtains were drawn, and Pippa found herself shifting from foot to foot, wanting to see inside.

Daphne fumbled through the ring until she held up a large iron key. 'Here we are,' she said, and, with difficulty, opened the door. 'It's probably best that we all go into the front room.'

Pippa followed the others into a sitting room which, while a period piece, was one from the 1980s rather than the 1880s. Striped wallpaper below, floral wallpaper above, and a toning stuck-on border. Black ash shelving, filled with copper ornaments and family sagas. China shepherdesses on top of the gas fire, and possibly the last non-flat-screen TV in Gadcestershire.

Jeremy Lightfoot gazed around him, clearly disappointed. 'I thought this was listed,' he said.

'It's Grade II,' said Daphne. 'That only covers the exterior.'

'Mmm,' said Jeremy. 'Won't you sit down, Lady Higginbotham?'

Lady Higginbotham looked at Daphne, who hastily said, 'Oh yes, do sit down everyone. I'll go and make tea.' She fled, and presently Pippa heard the opening rumble of a noisy kettle.

'I'm sure we shall find hidden treasure,' said Jeremy Lightfoot, pulling up his trouser knees and sitting gingerly on the overstuffed floral sofa.

The conversation lapsed, and Pippa found herself gazing about the room. Marge was right; she doubted any one outside Much Gadding, never mind international visitors, would queue to be admitted to Daphne's front room. *Not unless we marketed it as a museum to the eighties*, she thought, and turned a giggle into a cough.

After a few minutes Daphne returned bearing a tray with a teapot, cups and saucers, milk jug, and sugar bowl. Everything matched, and Pippa suspected that Daphne had got out her best china. 'Shall I be mother?' Daphne asked nervously. She reached for the teapot, and her hands trembled.

'I can do it if you like,' said Marge. 'A full teapot is heavy.'

Daphne's murmured thank-you was nearly inaudible. She sat in the corner of the sofa and folded herself small while Marge poured out.

'So, these letters,' said Jeremy Lightfoot, accepting a cup and stretching his legs out. 'May I see them?'

Daphne shot him a frightened glance. 'Yes, of course.' She got up and hurried from the room. *She seems almost guilty*, thought Pippa. *I wonder why?*

Daphne returned with a plain black ring-binder. Jeremy Lightfoot frowned, and stretched out his hand. 'I do hope they haven't been *mutilated*,' he said.

'Oh no,' said Daphne. 'I've put them in plastic wallets, to keep anything from getting on them.'

Jeremy Lightfoot opened the file. Each wallet held an envelope. 'Are the letters inside?' he asked.

'Yes,' said Daphne. 'It seemed best. For safekeeping.'

'May I...?' His hand hovered over the first wallet.

Daphne nodded. 'Please be careful,' she quavered.

Jeremy Lightfoot gave her a look which Pippa could only describe as contemptuous. 'I shall be very careful,' he said. Laying the file flat on the coffee table, he worked his long fingers into the plastic wallet, and secured the envelope. He glanced quickly at Daphne, and took the letter out. Then he took a pair of reading glasses from the breast pocket of his jacket, put them on, and read aloud.

Dear Phoebe,

Things are much the same here. Charles has a frightful cold as usual. I believe it is the damp climate. I am used to it, of course, but poor Charles is a martyr to his chest.

I would love to have you visit, but I'm afraid it is not possible at present. Charles is in no state to receive company, and our maid is the most slatternly drudge I ever set eyes on. I actually had to stand over her the other day to make sure she washed the china properly. At breakfast I found a smear of egg yolk on my plate which had clearly been there since the day before. I do declare that I don't know how they train these workhouse girls. I don't think the girl can even read; not more than simple words, at any rate.

Of course, this is most injurious to my writing. I sit at my desk and ponder, and between waiting for a crash from the scullery or a cough from Charles I find it impossible to concentrate. The cough will resolve itself soon, I am sure; but I doubt I can say the same for the housemaid.

I hope you and William are keeping well, and of course send all my love to darling Billy. Hopefully my next letter to you will be much more cheerful, as it must be if I receive one of your charming missives in the meantime.

Yours affectionately,
Clementina

'She sounds like a piece of work,' observed Marge.

Jeremy Lightfoot folded the letter back into its envelope. 'She is clearly writing to a dear friend,' he observed. 'Perhaps she is exaggerating the situation a little, and of course coping with creative frustration is extremely difficult.'

Marge snorted. 'It must be.'

'Could I look at some more of the letters?' asked Jeremy. 'Of course, the easiest way to accomplish that would be for me to perhaps borrow the file, and I could also get them reproduced—'

'I couldn't let you take the file,' said Daphne, quickly. 'They've been in my family for over a hundred years. I would never forgive myself if something happened to them —'

'Nothing would happen to them,' said Jeremy. 'I shall take the greatest care of them, and making copies would mean that the letters are preserved.' He peered at the envelope, which he still held. 'The ink here is beginning to fade. It is only a matter of time before these letters degrade so far that one could not preserve them.'

'Oh dear,' said Daphne.

'Well, that isn't going to happen tonight,' said Marge. 'So you don't need to make a decision about that yet, Daphne.'

Daphne brightened a little. 'Would you like to see her desk?' she said.

'You have her desk?' Jeremy Lightfoot pushed his sandy hair off his forehead. 'Why didn't you say?' He stood up. 'Where is it?'

'It's in the back bedroom,' said Daphne. She began to edge towards the door. 'But I must make sure the room is tidy first.' She gained the safety of the door, and vanished.

Jeremy Lightfoot smiled at the space where Daphne had been. 'It is an evening of surprises,' he remarked. 'Now, I wonder where the bathroom might be?'

'Up the stairs, straight ahead of you,' said Marge, rising. 'I'll show you.' She herded Jeremy Lightfoot out of the room like an efficient sheepdog.

Pippa leaned forward, and looked at the open file. The

next letter was addressed to Hoggins and Sons, Fleet Street, London. Presumably they were Clementina Stoate's publishers. She reached for the file, then stopped; she could hardly read the letter without Daphne's permission. Then she realised that her view of the envelope was uninterrupted. The letter which Jeremy Lightfoot had been reading was not in the file. *Hmm. I must make sure that is put back.* Jeremy had simply forgotten to replace it. Or at least, that was how she would choose to regard it for now.

Daphne returned, full of apologies. 'I was having a bit of a tidy,' she said, 'and – oh!' She glanced around wildly. 'Where is he?'

'He went to the bathroom,' said Pippa. 'Could I come and see?'

'Oh yes,' said Daphne, 'of course.'

Pippa followed her upstairs. Daphne opened the door of a small, plain room with a single bed, covered in a rose-sprigged counterpane. But its main feature was a large mahogany desk, bristling with drawers, with a green leather writing surface.

'Gosh,' said Pippa, 'that's impressive.'

'She left it to her niece in her will,' said Daphne, 'and it's stayed in the family ever since.' She looked conspiratorial. 'I don't think anyone felt they could get rid of it. The famous desk.' She opened the large central drawer, revealing neatly-folded pillowcases, then closed it hastily. 'I like the way it makes them smell,' she said, as if it were a weakness.

'I don't think she'd have minded,' said Pippa.

Daphne's eyes widened. 'I think she would,' she

replied. 'I think Clementina Stoate minded about lots of things.'

'Are all her letters like that?' asked Pippa.

Daphne shuffled her feet. 'Perhaps not all of them, but . . . quite a lot of them are.'

A tap at the door made Daphne jolt as if she had received an electric shock. 'Anybody home?' enquired Jeremy Lightfoot, sounding jocular. 'May I come in?'

'I'll go back downstairs,' said Pippa. 'I don't think there is space for more than two.'

'Oh, thank you,' said Daphne, with obvious relief.

As it turned out, Jeremy Lightfoot's train wasn't quite as urgent as he had first implied. It was half past nine before he looked at his watch and said, with great reluctance, that he really ought to go. Pippa had considered leaving several times; but somehow she felt a duty to Daphne to remain. The incident with the letter had unsettled her a little, and while Jeremy Lightfoot *had* replaced the letter in the file, she had seen his gaze stray towards it more than once.

To be fair, everyone had read a letter or two. After her initial reluctance, Daphne had unbent a little, and even giggled at one point. 'I don't think anyone would put her letters in print,' she said. 'All she writes about is the weather, her husband's health, and battles with her maid.'

Jeremy Lightfoot looked down his nose at her. 'I am sure that if one read all the letters, and carried out detailed textual analysis, then important themes would arise.'

Daphne raised her eyebrows. 'Would anyone like a biscuit?' She whisked off and returned with a Charles and

Diana biscuit tin filled with bourbons and custard creams.

It was one of the most surreal evenings Pippa had ever spent. People traipsed up and down the stairs to see Clementina Stoate's desk, and speculated over the contents of the letters, and every so often someone would nip to the bathroom. Norm had left at a quarter to nine, saying that he had book cataloguing to do at home; but Pippa happened to know that a police drama he watched began at nine o'clock.

But eventually everyone had seen the desk, had a second cup of tea and at least one biscuit, and Jeremy Lightfoot's departure was, apparently, imminent. 'Now where did I put my laptop bag?' he said, looking around in comic dismay. 'I definitely had it when I left the church hall—'

'Is it in the hallway?' said Pippa. 'That's where I usually put things when I know I'll need them soon.'

'That would make sense,' said Jeremy Lightfoot. He walked out of the room, then returned. 'No, I don't see it there, just the projector. I didn't take it upstairs, did I?'

'That seems unlikely,' Marge said. 'I'll go and see.'

'Oh no, I'll go,' said Daphne. 'You save your legs, Marge.'

'There is nothing wrong with my legs,' growled Marge. 'You stay here and see to Mr Lightfoot.' But Daphne had already scurried off.

'Did you put it near where you were sitting?' asked Lady Higginbotham, craning her neck to peer down the side of the sofa.

'Oh dear,' said Jeremy Lightfoot, looking worried. 'It is

password-protected, of course, and I hope everything is backed up, but I do have the edits for my new book on there—'

'Then we must find it,' said Lady Higginbotham. She rose and began to take the cushions off the sofa, though it would have been next to impossible for any laptop to work its way behind those.

Daphne re-entered the room. 'No, it isn't anywhere upstairs,' she said, then flinched as Lady Higginbotham threw another cushion on the floor. 'Oh dear me.'

'Could it be outside?' said Pippa. 'You might have put it down while we waited for the door to be opened, and then in your excitement—'

'It's possible,' said Jeremy Lightfoot. 'Would you mind checking?' He patted his pockets. 'Now I definitely have my wallet, and my train ticket…'

After everyone had inspected every nook and cranny, Jeremy Lightfoot's laptop was eventually found beneath the frilled valance of the sofa where he had been sitting. 'Of course!' he exclaimed. 'I remember now, I tucked it under there so that it would be out of the way.' He slung the large bag over his shoulder. 'Now I know I left the projector in the hallway.' He smiled at Daphne, who looked ten years older. 'Would you happen to have the number of a reliable taxi firm?'

Once Jeremy Lightfoot had been waved off, with many assurances that he would give Clementina Stoate his undivided attention, Marge shooed everyone else from the house. 'Daphne's had enough for one evening,' she said, scowling. 'I'm sure that Mr Lightfoot will be in touch with

us all promptly. Especially if he wants us to do anything.'
She gave Pippa a significant glance.

Pippa didn't go straight home, but stopped at the village green and sat on the bench. *What a strange evening*, she thought. Was it possible that Clementina Stoate would become a local literary celebrity? She remembered the letter, and giggled. *I wonder what her maid thought of her.*

The church clock began to chime the hour. *Better go home*, she thought, reluctantly rising. *At least we only have to look after ourselves.*

Chapter 5

Pippa's phone buzzed. *Pick up Ruby*, the reminder said.

Pippa sighed. 'There's never enough time,' she said. She had spent much of her newly available Wednesday afternoon getting Jeff's email under control, only pausing when she felt her finger automatically reaching for the delete button. After that she had engaged in marquee negotiations. The new quotes, as she had suspected, were considerably more reasonable, so she had contacted their usual supplier to suggest they reconsider their price.

She had also received an email from Lady Higginbotham. Not about the Proms, or the holiday cottages, but the literary festival. *Should we get quotes done? Mr Lightfoot hopes to secure funding, and it would be helpful to have a realistic estimate ready for him, wouldn't it? If you have any time, Pippa, it would be wonderful if you could put something together.*

Wouldn't it, thought Pippa, and closed the email. She was still unsure about the idea of the Clementina Stoate-a-thon, in any case. Yes, it was another event to put Much

Gadding on the map. But was there enough material to build a festival on? *If only Agatha Christie had lived here. Or even stayed for a weekend. I could have made a proper festival out of that.*

Her phone buzzed again. *Go NOW*, it said. And Pippa obeyed.

She rang the nursery doorbell and plastered on her best smile. Alicia came to the door, and through the glass panel, Pippa could immediately see her wary expression. *Oh no.*

'Hello, Mrs Parker,' said Alicia. 'Ruby is in the Cygnet Room today.'

Pippa's heart sank as she followed Alicia in. She knocked on the door, and was admitted by a small, dark young woman she hadn't spoken to before. Her name badge said she was Tasha.

'Hello, Tasha,' she said. 'I'm Pippa Parker, here to pick up Ruby. How has she been?' She looked around the room for Ruby. There were more children in the room than she was used to – of course there would be – and she searched for Ruby's dark curls. *What clothes did I put her in this morning?*

Tasha scrutinised Pippa. 'Well, it was her first day in here today, and... There she is.' Ruby was sitting in a corner, with another helper that Pippa didn't know. 'How has Ruby been, Rach?'

Rach got to her feet and offered Ruby a hand, but Ruby shook her head. 'Look, there's Mummy!' Rach said, pointing.

Ruby appeared disbelieving, then saw Pippa, and ran to

her. 'Mummy, Mummy!' she cried, throwing her arms round Pippa's leg.

'Up you come.' Pippa lifted Ruby and sat her on her hip.

'It was a bit much for her,' said Rach. 'A lot of the children in on Wednesdays are quite big. They did ask Ruby to play, but she didn't want to. She's been sitting in the corner by herself most of the afternoon. Oh, and – excuse me a moment.' She went to a cupboard and produced a carrier bag which she handed to Pippa. 'I'm afraid she had a little accident.'

'Really?' That wasn't like Ruby at all.

'It's early days,' said Rach soothingly. 'She'll probably be fine in a week.'

'Yes, hopefully,' said Pippa, cuddling Ruby closer. Ruby snuggled in, and she felt terrible. 'Right, trouble, let's go and get Freddie.'

'Do I come tomorrow?' asked Ruby, looking worried.

'No, it's playgroup tomorrow,' said Pippa. 'You'll have me all day.'

'Good,' said Ruby, tightening her grip.

They went to fetch Freddie, and then Pippa read stories with Ruby on the sofa, while Freddie played with his toy garage on the rug. *I ought to be thinking about dinner,* she thought, between books.

Ruby needs you, her inner voice said. *She's probably had a rotten time today. Dinner can wait.* Pippa gave them milk and biscuits as a stopgap, and a mug of tea for herself. Not that she required any caffeine; she felt buzzy enough as it was.

And speaking of buzz… She picked her phone up from the coffee table. *You have a new email.*

Pippa clicked on the message, then groaned. It was from Jeremy Lightfoot.

Dear Mrs Parker (may I call you Pippa?)

It was lovely to meet you at the meeting in Much Gadding yesterday. It went extremely well, and I certainly made some surprising discoveries. I also thought your questions about the practicalities of the festival showed great insight.

Here we go, thought Pippa.

I wondered, Pippa, if I might ask a small favour. The short glimpse I managed to catch of Clementina Stoate's letters was absolutely fascinating, and I feel sure there is a great deal of valuable material there, if only I could manage to look at it properly. I have attempted to contact Daphne and request a further viewing, but she doesn't seem to be answering her phone.

Could you find it in your heart to act as an intermediary and have a chat with her? Please assure her that I have no intention of taking the letters from her. Of course it would make the most sense to get the letters scanned professionally, but even taking pictures with my phone would be better than nothing.

If you could do that, and let me know how you get on, it would be immensely helpful. Of course, any applications for funding will have a much greater chance of success

with a coup such as new unpublished material to reveal.
Many thanks for your help,
Jeremy Lightfoot

'Oh,' said Pippa. Both the children looked at her, and she realised she had spoken out loud.

'What's up, Mummy?' said Freddie. 'Is it work?'

'Sort of,' said Pippa. 'Someone wants me to do something for him.'

'Do you work for him?' asked Freddie.

'Um, no,' said Pippa.

'Say no,' said Ruby.

'It isn't as easy as that,' said Pippa. 'I may work for him in the future, if I do what he asks, but I don't have time.'

'Ruby's right,' said Freddie. 'You should say no. Then you can play with us. What's for tea?'

'I don't know,' said Pippa. 'I haven't thought about that yet.'

***

Simon came home to find Pippa eyeing the oven. 'What's on the menu chez Parker?' he asked.

'Fish fingers, chips and peas for the kids. Chicken Kiev, chips, and random veg for us when they're in bed,' she replied, still watching the oven. 'That do you?'

'Has it been one of those days?' he asked.

'It has,' said Pippa. 'Ruby had her first day in the Cygnets today, and it didn't go well.'

'Oh dear,' said Simon. 'But it's only her first day. She'll probably be fine after a couple more goes.'

'That's pretty much what Rach said,' Pippa replied.

'But she had an accident, and that isn't like her. You know how quickly we potty trained her, compared with Freddie.'

'It's probably just one of those things,' said Simon.

But when Pippa served the children's tea, Ruby demanded that hers was cut up for her.

'But you like cutting up your food,' said Pippa.

'No I don't,' said Ruby, folding her arms. 'Cut it up, Mummy.'

'No,' said Pippa.

Ruby thrust out her bottom lip and stared at her plate, and two minutes later, Pippa found herself slicing fish fingers and chips into easily manageable chunks. Ruby grinned in triumph, shot out a hand, and put a chunk of fish finger into her mouth.

'Ruby!' said Simon. 'Use your fork.'

'Don't want to,' said Ruby, grabbing a chip.

Then Freddie picked a chip up, too.

'Don't you start,' warned Pippa. 'Use your knife and fork, both of you, or else no pudding.'

Freddie hastily picked up his fork, but Ruby continued to shovel food into her mouth with her hands.

Simon was waiting with a glass of wine when Pippa came down from tucking the children in. 'I begin to see what you mean,' he said.

'She was really clingy earlier, too,' said Pippa. 'I don't think she's ready. But I've got this extra work to do for Jeff, and then there's this stupid festival – and Jeremy Lightfoot wants me to do his dirty work for him.'

'Just say no,' said Simon. 'If he doesn't pay, he doesn't get your time.'

'I get that,' said Pippa. 'But if I don't help, and because of that the festival doesn't happen, then I'll feel bad. And what if Ruby does settle, and I do have time on my hands, and I've lost the opportunity?'

Simon sighed. 'What does he want you to do, anyway?'

He pushed the glass across the table and Pippa drank some wine before answering. 'It's nothing much,' she said. 'He wants me to ask Daphne – she's Clementina's descendant – to let him see the letters again. He's tried phoning, but she didn't answer.'

'That doesn't sound too hard,' said Simon. 'Couldn't you pop round and see if she's up for it? I'm sure you could sell it to her. Then Jeremy Lightfoot can crack on, and he'll owe you a favour when the time comes for actual paid work.'

'You're right,' said Pippa, taking another sip of wine. 'Have you put the food in yet?'

'Does that mean you want to go now?' Simon asked.

'Might do,' admitted Pippa. 'It's still early, and she'll probably be in. And if I can sort this out, at least I'll have achieved something today.'

Pippa changed back into her black trousers and put on a slightly smarter top before walking to Daphne's cottage. *It might be better for her if he did take the letters*, she thought. *Much less bother, and people wouldn't need to come to the cottage. We could keep it out of the festival altogether.*

Yes, that was obviously the best thing. She smiled, and gave the brass door knocker a smart tap.

Daphne looked surprised to see her, but not scared or

worried, which Pippa took as a good sign. 'Hello,' she said, opening the door wider. 'Is it Pippa?'

'That's right,' said Pippa. 'I wondered how you were after our meeting the other day.'

'Oh yes,' Daphne let out a fragile, tinkling laugh. 'That was rather an occasion, wasn't it?' The door opened wider still. 'Marge told me about you, once everyone had left. I didn't know you helped the police.'

'Oh, I do sometimes,' said Pippa, trying to make that sound perfectly normal.

'You look as if you want to speak to me,' said Daphne.

'Um, yes,' said Pippa. 'Could I come in for a few minutes?'

Five minutes later she was sitting on the floral sofa, with a cup of tea in front of her, and a bourbon biscuit tucked into the saucer. 'You see, Daphne, I've had an email from Jeremy Lightfoot.'

Daphne shuddered. 'Oh no.'

'No, no, it isn't anything bad. He just wondered if he could come and see the letters properly, because he found them so interesting.'

'I don't think that's a good idea,' said Daphne.

'Oh, but it is,' said Pippa. 'The thing is, if he takes pictures of them while he's here, then he doesn't have to bother you again. Or you could get them digitised, and then no one would bother you.'

'But they would bother me,' said Daphne. 'They'd ask me why it hadn't been done before, or they'd want to see the desk, or go round the house, or open up the house, or have cream teas in the house—'

Pippa laughed. 'I'm not sure there would be room for cream teas in the house, Daphne. There would be much more space at Higginbotham Hall.'

'That's true,' said Daphne. 'And I know I would much rather have a cream tea there.'

'Lady Higginbotham is keen to help,' said Pippa. 'That would take the strain off you.'

'Is she?' said Daphne. 'That's good of her.'

'Yes,' said Pippa. 'So if you said yes to Jeremy Lightfoot popping in one day—'

'Oh no, I can't,' said Daphne.

Pippa stared at her. 'But you said—'

'No, I absolutely can't,' said Daphne. 'And there's nothing I can do about that. You see…' She looked around the room, then back to Pippa. 'The letters aren't here any more,' she whispered. 'They've gone.'

Chapter 6

'What do you mean, gone?' said Pippa. She realised she was holding her cup at a dangerous tilt, and put it hurriedly onto the saucer. The rattle made Daphne jump.

'Yes, they have,' she said, sounding more sure of herself. 'The letters have gone.'

'How? When? When did you notice?'

Daphne drew back slightly. 'Um, not straight away. I mean, it was such a busy evening, with everyone in here, and then going upstairs to see the desk, and using the bathroom, and hunting for Mr Lightfoot's laptop—'

'So when did you notice that the letters were gone?' Pippa repeated.

'Not until today,' said Daphne. 'You see, Marge helped me to get things straight afterwards. I assumed she had just put the file away.'

'Where are they usually kept?' asked Pippa. 'Would Marge know?'

'I don't think I've ever told her,' said Daphne. 'She might have seen me take them out, I suppose. But she was so helpful. She talked to me afterwards, and said I must make sure not to be bullied by Mr Lightfoot. Or is he Dr Lightfoot? I'm not sure.'

'Never mind that now,' said Pippa. 'So when did you realise the letters had gone missing?'

'When I was doing my housework,' said Daphne. 'I always do my housework on the same day, you see. I normally keep the letters in Clementina's desk, because that seems like a logical place to put them. Normally I wouldn't even check, but something made me this time, and they weren't there.'

Pippa considered. 'So the whole file of letters has gone?'

'Yes,' said Daphne. 'All of it. The whole thing.'

'And you're sure they haven't been put back in the wrong place? As you say, you don't think Marge knows where you keep them.' Pippa surveyed Daphne's somewhat cramped sitting room. 'She could easily have left them in the bookshelf.'

'I've looked everywhere,' said Daphne. 'And they definitely aren't there.'

'I see,' said Pippa. 'Have you asked Marge when she remembers seeing them, or whether she put them somewhere out of the way?'

Daphne's hands twisted in her lap. 'If I did, she'd know the letters were missing, and she'd worry. She might think that I thought she'd…'

'But you do want to find them, don't you?' asked Pippa.

Daphne was silent for some time. 'To be absolutely honest,' she said, quietly, 'I'm not sure I do.'

'But she's your ancestor!' cried Pippa. 'You wouldn't let Jeremy Lightfoot have the letters because you were worried something might happen to them!'

'Oh, please don't tell Jeremy Lightfoot that the letters are missing!' Daphne wrung her hands. 'He'd call the police, and come and interrogate me, and it would be awful.' She stared at Pippa with wide, pale-blue eyes. 'And you can't tell the police, either. I can't bear the thought of them poking round my house, and asking why I didn't take better care of the letters— And I have taken care of them,' she said. 'Until Mr Lightfoot came they were perfectly safe, and no one cared about them. Well, except Marge.'

'Oh,' said Pippa. 'I thought she wasn't a fan of Clementina Stoate.'

'No, she isn't,' said Daphne. 'But her niece Briony teaches at the University of Gadcester. I think she specialises in that sort of thing. Marge has been saying for ages that I ought to let her have a look.'

'I see,' said Pippa, her mind whirling. How come, in the time that she'd known Marge, she'd never even mentioned that she had a niece, much less an academic one? 'That hardly matters now, I suppose, since the letters are missing.' She picked up her biscuit and bit into it, chewing slowly to give herself time. 'This alters the purpose of my visit somewhat,' she said.

'I suppose it does,' said Daphne. 'I am sorry, dear. I didn't mean to cause trouble.'

'No, of course you haven't,' said Pippa, feeling guilty. *This poor woman has lost part of her history*, she thought. *She must feel terrible, after guarding it so carefully for all this time.* 'Is there anything I can do to help?'

Daphne stared at her. 'But how?'

'Well,' said Pippa, 'I help the police sometimes. If you don't want to call the police in, perhaps I could do some very quiet investigating and try to find the letters.'

The moment she had said it she cursed herself inwardly. *What were you saying about being too busy? And here you are taking on a solo investigation.*

'Oh no, you really don't have to—' said Daphne, looking wretched.

'I can't promise anything,' said Pippa. 'But I can try my best.' She checked her watch. 'Good heavens, I said I'd only be a few minutes.' She stood up. 'I must head home now, but I'll be back in touch soon. Apart from anything else, I need to make sure I've got the details of the evening right. I'll bring a notepad, and write down what you tell me.'

'That sounds official,' said Daphne warily.

'It's not as official as it would be if the police called you to the station to do it,' remarked Pippa.

Daphne shivered. 'Very well then, dear, I suppose I must do as you say.'

***

Pippa hurried home, grateful for the cool evening air after Daphne's stuffy sitting room. *Who could have taken the letters?* Her first thought had been Jeremy Lightfoot. He had shown great interest in the letters, he clearly wanted to inspect them more closely, and he had created all that bother over his missing laptop and got everyone searching for it. The perfect opportunity to take the file –

but then why would he have urged Pippa to go and see Daphne about the letters? That would draw attention to their disappearance.

And now there was the problem of Marge. Marge, who had been so insistent that Daphne shouldn't give the letters to Jeremy Lightfoot, but had helped her tidy up afterwards. Could she have taken them?

Pippa shook her head as soon as she thought it; but the thought wouldn't go. Marge had a motive, and an opportunity, and moreover she was someone whom Daphne trusted. 'Oh dear,' said Pippa out loud. She looked around guiltily to see if anyone had heard her, but the street was deserted.

'Did you win?' asked Simon, once Pippa had let herself in. He was leaning on the worktop and watching the oven, much as Pippa had earlier.

'Not exactly,' said Pippa. 'Don't tell anyone, but the letters have gone missing.'

'Really?' Simon whistled. 'Blimey. Are you going to ring Jim Horsley?'

'No,' said Pippa. 'I am not going to ring Jim Horsley. For one thing, Jim doesn't work in Much Gadding any more, he works in Gadcester. And secondly, Daphne won't report it.'

'Does that mean you're on the case?' asked Simon.

'I don't think I have a choice,' said Pippa. 'But I'm not doing anything until I've had my dinner. If it wasn't one of those days before, it definitely is now.'

***

After dinner, while ostensibly watching the latest

episode of a drama series, Pippa sat next to Simon with her notepad, and thought.

First she wrote the names of everyone who had attended the meeting. *Jeremy Lightfoot, Daphne, Lady Higginbotham, Malcolm Allison, Norm, Marge, me.* She supposed that everyone whom Jeremy had invited had come, since he hadn't waited any longer once Lady Higginbotham had arrived. Then again, she reflected, Lady Higginbotham was probably the most important person there, as far as he was concerned.

And Marge wasn't meant to be there. Daphne had invited her, presumably because she was worried about not being able to stand up to Jeremy Lightfoot. And Marge had helped. *But it might have helped her too.*

Who else had a motive to take the letters? *Obviously not me*, thought Pippa. *I've got enough to do without puzzling over the loopy handwriting of a minor poet.* Norm could be safely counted out too. His interests leant much more towards thrillers and current affairs. Malcolm Allison? Pippa doubted it. His interest in history went much further back. But then she remembered the magpie-like tendencies he had shown during another case, and the strange array of miscellaneous objects in his house. Was it possible that he had been left alone with the letters, and saw an opportunity? 'But where would he have put them?'

Simon gave her an exasperated look. 'If you're not watching this, you could go in the other room.'

'Sorry,' said Pippa. 'I am trying. But I've got a lot on my mind.'

He sighed, and paused the TV. 'Cuppa?'

'I'll make it,' said Pippa. 'You carry on.'

She went into the kitchen and dropped teabags into mugs. Like it or not, Malcolm could be a possible. What about Lady Higginbotham? But what on earth would she do with the letters? Then Pippa considered. Lady Higginbotham was keen on having the literary festival at the hall. Normally, if something was stolen, the owner would report it, and there might be a public appeal. Could she possibly have taken the letters with the intention of raising publicity? It didn't seem like her; but sometimes Lady H had odd ideas.

And then, of course, there was Jeremy Lightfoot. The man who wanted to set himself up as a Clementina Stoate expert. The publicity argument would work as far as he was concerned, too, thought Pippa, with a sense of satisfaction. And he would have a head start on working with the letters, since no other academic had had a sniff of them. Plus he had pushed to go to Daphne's cottage, and created that massive diversion—

The kettle pinged, and Pippa made the tea.

'Thanks,' said Simon, not taking his eyes off the screen. 'Have you solved it yet?'

Pippa laughed. 'Not quite,' she said. 'But it's rather worrying. There are a lot more people with a reason to take the letters than I thought.'

'Mmm,' said Simon. 'Maybe you should ring Jim.'

'For the last time,' said Pippa, 'I am not ringing Jim. I am perfectly capable of managing this on my own.'

'I didn't say you weren't,' said Simon.

'You implied it,' said Pippa.

Simon looked across at her, eyebrows raised. 'Someone's touchy,' he said.

'Perhaps someone who has solved five far more serious cases thinks that finding some missing letters is hardly the greatest challenge of her detective career.' Pippa stood up. 'You carry on watching your programme, I'm going upstairs to think.'

Pippa flounced upstairs with her notebook and tea. She tried to remember where everyone had been sitting at Daphne's, but they had moved around. And was the file on the table all that time? Who had picked it up?

I'll have to talk to people, she thought. *This is ridiculous. I'm going round in circles.*

Then a thought struck her. What if someone had read a letter and found it contained something important? Would that have made them take the file? *I'll try to read some of the letters*, she thought. Jeremy Lightfoot knew of twelve of them, so they must be published somewhere. *I'll check the library catalogue tomorrow, and if Gadcester Library has anything about Clementina Stoate, I'll borrow it. At least that's a start.*

Pippa wrote herself a note, underlined it, and reached for her tea with satisfaction. There. She had already taken a gulp before she realised it was stone cold.

Chapter 7

After playgroup, and a somewhat hasty lunch of ham sandwiches, Pippa buckled Ruby into her car seat and drove to Gadcester.

'Is it the bookshop, Mummy?' asked Ruby.

'Not this time,' said Pippa.

'Not the museum, Mummy,' pleaded Ruby.

'No,' agreed Pippa. 'Not the museum. We're going to the library.'

She could see Ruby's confused little face in the rear-view mirror. 'But library's at home.'

'This is a different library,' said Pippa, firmly. 'It has different books.' *And hopefully*, she thought, *if the online catalogue is right, it has the book I want.*

'Children's books?' asked Ruby.

'I should think so,' said Pippa.

'Read to me, Mummy.'

'Yes,' said Pippa. 'But only if you're good, and you let me find my book first. We need to be back in time to pick up Freddie.'

Pippa managed to find a parking spot fairly quickly, got a ticket, then lifted Ruby out of her seat. 'I want to waaaaalk,' said Ruby.

'I'm sure you do,' said Pippa, 'but I want to hurry. You can walk on the way back, if you like.'

Ruby wriggled like a fish out of water then began to buck, until Pippa put her down with an exasperated sigh and took hold of her hand. 'Do you know, Ruby, sometimes I miss the days when I could strap you in and wheel you about.'

Ruby stared up at her. 'You said you wanted to hurry.'

Restraining a swearword, Pippa set off for the library.

She hadn't been in Gadcester Library for a while. Partly because it involved a car journey and paying to park, partly because the book selection was, if anything, less to her taste than that of Much Gadding, but also out of a sense of loyalty. Norm, she felt, needed her custom in a way that this library did not.

As she had expected, it was busy. Many of the patrons were of pensionable age. Some, mainly men, were sitting at tables reading the papers, while women with shoppers on wheels trundled them from aisle to aisle, peering at shelves. However, there was also a group of younger women with children; mainly in pushchairs, but some Ruby's age and a few preschoolers. They were huddled in the children's area in an expectant manner.

'Look,' said Ruby, pointing. 'Something's happening. Can I see?'

And it was. The librarian came over with a chair and a book, and placed it on the rug, which was the signal for a stampede by the toddlers to sit nearest to her, and much manoeuvring of pushchairs by the mums.

A cunning plan entered Pippa's head. 'The librarian is going to read a book, Ruby. Would you like to hear the story?'

Ruby didn't answer, but shot off to the rug, dropped to her knees, and crawled through to a small space near the front.

Excellent, thought Pippa. Keeping her eyes on Ruby, she moved back, glancing about her every so often in search of shelf markers for poetry. The library catalogue had listed a *Selected Poems of Clementina Stoate*, and mentioned an appendix of letters. Pippa kept edging away from the children's section, having to dodge advancing pushchairs every so often, until she was close to the enquiry desk. The librarian was busy stamping a pile of Mary Wesleys for an elderly lady, and Pippa waited patiently while the borrower discoursed on the inadequacies of the bus service.

At length it was her turn. 'Excuse me, could you tell me where I would find the selected poems of Clementina Stoate?'

The librarian frowned. 'Poems, you say? Those come under literature. In that corner, next to Young Adult.'

'Thanks,' said Pippa, and hurried across the library, almost getting tangled up with an unattended tartan shopper on wheels on the way.

The literature section was not large, mostly consisting of Penguin Classics. Pippa's gaze roved over the shelves. *Novels . . . Plays...*

'Poetry!' she cried, and dropped to her knees, for the poetry section was on the bottom shelf. Auden, Browning, Coleridge... *Come on, Pippa.*

Wordsworth . . . Yeats... *Damn, too far!*

Then she spotted it; a slim red hardback with *C. Stoate – Poems* stamped in gold on the spine. She pulled it out, and opened it to the title page.

Selected Poems of Clementina Stoate, with an Appendix of Selected Letters. Edited by P. Onions, late of the University of London. Beneath was the date; 1936.

Pippa closed the book and hurried back to the children's section. Ruby was still sitting where Pippa had left her, completely engrossed. 'Thank you,' Pippa breathed, to the librarian rather than any higher deity, and waited for the story to finish.

As it turned out, the librarian was on the last page. 'And they all lived happily ever after,' she concluded. 'The end.'

A collective 'Ooooohhhh' rose from the rug, followed by cries of 'Another one! Another one!'

Yes please, thought Pippa.

The librarian surveyed the occupants of the rug severely. 'Have you been good enough to deserve another story?' she enquired.

All the children who were capable nodded frantically.

'Very well,' said the librarian. 'In that case, I shall read you another.' She leaned to her right and pulled out another book from a box on the floor, then showed it to her audience. 'Does anyone know who this is?'

'Elmer!' shouted a few voices.

'That's right, it's Elmer. Let's see what he gets up to.'

She opened the book, settled her glasses more comfortably on her nose, cleared her throat, and began to read.

Yes, thought Pippa, and, not even pretending to be interested in the story, headed to the desk once more. Luckily this time no one was waiting. 'Could I take this out, please?' she asked, putting the red book on the counter.

The librarian peered at the book as if she'd never seen anything like it in her life. 'Clementina Stoate,' she read, before opening it. 'That rings a bell.'

'Oh really?' asked Pippa, as casually as she could manage. 'Why would that be?'

'Do you have your library card?'

Pippa fumbled in her purse, extracting various loyalty cards, membership cards, and even a long-defunct Blockbuster Video card, before finding the right one and handing it over. 'Here you are,' she said. 'So you said it rang a bell?'

'Mmm,' said the librarian. 'I've never seen anyone take this out until perhaps a fortnight ago.'

'That's a funny coincidence,' said Pippa. 'Who took it out?'

The librarian's expression was deadpan. 'I don't have a photographic memory of everyone who borrows a book, you know,' she said. 'That's what the computer's for.'

'I'm sorry,' said Pippa, feeling rather frustrated. 'I just wondered, seeing as you said it had never been taken out.'

'I don't know about never,' said the librarian. 'I mean, I've only been working here for five years.' She picked up her stamp, and positioned it ready. 'Looking at this, the lady who had it before you was the first to take it out in ten years.' The stamp went down with a decisive clunk. 'Back in three weeks, please.'

'Wow,' said Pippa. 'And now me.'

'Yes,' said the librarian meditatively. 'I hadn't realised she was local until the other lady told me. She said this Cordelia Stoate—'

'Clementina,' Pippa corrected automatically.

The librarian checked the title page. 'Oh yes, you're right. This Stoate woman lived in Much Gadding, quite near where her aunt lives.'

'Good heavens,' said Pippa, 'I had no idea.'

'No,' said the librarian, and mused for a moment. 'It's nice to think we have a local author. I mean an old-established one, I know there are others.' She thought again. 'But neither of you look like the sort to borrow poetry. Usually it's either young people dressed in black or chaps in tweed jackets. And *they* normally want Kipling.'

'Oh, I see,' said Pippa. 'No, I don't suppose either one of us fits into those categories.'

'Not really,' said the librarian. 'She had red hair – sort of studenty red – and big boots. I thought she was a student, but her library card said she was a doctor.' She shrugged. 'It takes all sorts.'

'Doesn't it,' said Pippa. Then she heard a small hullabaloo coming from the children's library. 'I'd better go and fetch my little girl; story time has finished.'

'Oh, there'll be one more yet,' said the librarian. 'She always does three.'

Storing that fact away for another day, Pippa wandered

back to the children's section, and flicked through the pages of the red book. She glanced at poem after poem, but nothing from them sank in. She was too busy thinking about the person who had borrowed the book before her. A red-haired woman who looked like a student, and was almost certainly Marge's niece. Wouldn't she own a copy of the book anyway? Obviously not, or she wouldn't have borrowed one. Judging by the lack of interest in Clementina Stoate, this might be the most recent collection of her work, and it wasn't a mass-market edition.

The third story was shorter, and within five minutes Pippa was pulled onto a beanbag and presented with a selection of books to read to Ruby, among them another Elmer book and *Not Now, Bernard*. Pippa half-wondered whether that was suitable for a toddler, but Ruby loved it and demanded a second reading. In fact, they read so many books that it was only when Pippa caught sight of the clock that she realised they would have to get a move on.

'Come on, Ruby,' she said, getting up in a most undignified manner. 'We must go, or I'll be late for school.'

'But your book, Mummy,' said Ruby.

'Don't worry,' said Pippa. 'I got it while you were listening to stories.'

Ruby looked put out. 'Didn't you watch me listening?'

'Oh, I could still see you,' said Pippa. 'And I could tell you were listening ever so well.'

Ruby smiled. 'Let's go, Mummy!' she said, putting her hand into Pippa's. 'Can we come back?'

'I don't see why not,' said Pippa. After all, she

reflected, there were days when fifteen or twenty minutes of keeping Ruby occupied in a way that didn't involve her would be absolutely wonderful. And she picked up a Story Time leaflet on the way out of the library. *But before we come back*, she thought, *I'm going to find out more about the mysterious redheaded woman. And hopefully, she and I will have a little chat.*

Chapter 8

Pippa found herself driving back to Gadcester the very next morning.

A search on the staff page at the University of Gadcester had revealed no young women called Briony, or any remotely like the person the librarian had *described. None of their research interests matched, either. Maybe the website hasn't been updated*, thought Pippa, *or she isn't a permanent member of staff. I'll have to throw the net a bit wider.*

She returned to her search engine and typed in *Dr Briony University Gadcester.*

Aha! Now we're getting somewhere! She scrolled down the list, which seemed to be mostly titles. 'A reappraisal of Christina Rossetti': Dr Briony Shepherd, University of Gadcester.

'So she does exist,' murmured Pippa. Next she typed *Briony Shepherd* into the search engine and looked for images. 'There you are!' she cried. A woman with short, bright-red hair stared back at the camera, arms folded. She was leaning on an oak-panelled door, wearing a black T-shirt, jeans, and Doc Martens.

Now, how can I get in touch with you? She didn't look like the sort of person who would be on Facebook. Pippa typed *Briony Shepherd Twitter*.

Briony Shepherd was on there, with the username @VictorianLantern. Pippa was about to click the link when she had a sudden thought. She opened up a new, incognito window in her browser, searched again, and this time clicked through.

Briony had 15,000 followers, and followed 1000 people. *She's popular*, thought Pippa. Her bio said: *Reappraising the Victorians one text at a time. Will theorise for money. She/her*. Pippa clicked on the link in the bio, and found a no-frills blog headed The Victorian Lantern. It overflowed with entries; articles on Victorian advertisements, Victorian poetry, and modern TV adaptations of Victorian books. Pippa read with increasing bewilderment. *Why are these stuck on a blog?*

The answer came quickly. *Because she isn't a name. Because an opportunity like speaking at a literary festival, or getting to work on Clementina Stoate's poems, could be just the lift she needs.*

The blog had a contact form. Pippa thought for a moment, then decided to take the plunge.

Dear Briony, she wrote,

I came across you on Twitter and I've been reading the articles on your blog, which I found fascinating.

I am currently in talks to organise a small event about

Clementina Stoate in Much Gadding, the place where she lived. We shall be looking for speakers. At this stage I should say that nothing is definite, but I'd be most interested in having a conversation with you.

Kind regards,
Pippa Parker

Pippa typed her email address in the box and pressed *Send*.

A reply came into her inbox within fifteen minutes.

Dear Pippa,

Thanks for taking the time to write to me. I'd be keen to learn more about this event. We can chat on email if you like, or if you'd prefer to meet in person, I have an hour free tomorrow between 10 and 11. My office is room 309B in the Modern Languages Building at the University of Gadcester.

Looking forward to hearing more,
Briony

She's keen, thought Pippa. *Then again, why wouldn't she be? This is her sort of thing. She's probably hoping that I can succeed where her aunt has failed.* Feeling just a little Machiavellian, she hit *Reply*.

Dear Briony,

Thanks for your prompt reply. I think an in-person chat would work better, so I'll take you up on tomorrow morning.

See you soon,
Pippa

Simon put his head round the dining-room door. 'I was going to offer you tea, but you look like the cat who got the cream,' he said.

'I'm meeting Marge's niece tomorrow morning,' said Pippa. 'I've just set it up.'

'Um, congratulations?' said Simon.

'She's an academic who does Victorian poetry,' said Pippa. 'She could be a lead. Or give me a lead.'

'OK,' said Simon. 'I also came in to tell you that it's ten o'clock, and I kind of miss you.'

'Sorry,' said Pippa. 'But I didn't have time to do anything until the kids were in bed, and you complain if I do stuff like this in the same room as you…'

'The police are there for a reason,' said Simon.

'Maybe so,' said Pippa, 'but this isn't a police matter. And yes, a cup of tea would be lovely.'

Simon tutted, and disappeared.

Pippa looked at the doorway where he had been, sighed, and closed the laptop. Now she had tracked Briony down and organised a meeting, she could sleep easy. But what on earth should she wear?

***

The Modern Languages Building was well-signposted and easy to find. Room 309B, however, was a different matter. Pippa had walked up and down the corridor twice; 308, 309, 310, but no 309B. In the end she stopped a harassed-looking young man striding along with a pile of books. 'Excuse me, where would I find room 309B, please?'

The pile of books began to teeter. He sandwiched it between his hands, then gave her a reproachful glance. 'OK, go past room 312, then there's another door without a label. Go through that, and 309B is on your left.' He was gone before Pippa had the chance to thank him.

Easy when you know how, thought Pippa, arriving outside room 309B. She checked her watch: 9.58. No noise came from within the room, so she knocked, but there was no answer. She looked at the door. While the other doors had had nameplates, this one had a printed sheet of A4 attached: *Dr Briony Shepherd*. Beneath was scribbled: *Office hours: 9 to 5 most days, 9 to 3 Wednesdays. If you want to see me, and you can't hear talking, knock.* Around the notice were blu-tacked a range of pictures. Some were paintings of women in Victorian-looking dress, while others were printouts of Victorian advertisements, or playbills, or cartoons.

Then she heard approaching footsteps – not one set, but several – and a string of seemingly random questions:

'Can I talk to you about my essay, Briony?'

'Which edition of *The Merchant of Venice* would you recommend? The library has five different ones, and I'm not sure which to choose.'

'Um, could you give me a reference? It's for a job—'

A loud, decided voice cut in. 'I can deal with all those things, but not now, as I have a meeting. Can you either email me or come to the office at one, please.'

A collective, ragged 'Ohhh' rose, which reminded

Pippa of the toddlers on the library rug the day before.

'I can't always be on tap,' said the voice. 'I do have other things to do.'

The door to the main corridor opened and Pippa saw an assortment of students. They shambled off, eyeing Pippa as they went, without interest. They were dressed in a variety of styles, but all looked absurdly young. *That means I'm getting old*, thought Pippa.

Behind them was a face and head of hair that Pippa recognised. 'Hello,' said Briony Shepherd. 'You must be Pippa.'

'That's right,' said Pippa. 'And you must be Briony.'

'Yup,' said Briony, unlocking the door. 'Come in. Coffee?'

'Yes please,' said Pippa. She followed Briony into the room, which was small and cramped. Much of the space was taken up by bookshelves. In the corner was a small desk with a computer, piled with papers. Above it was a board covered with flyers and notices.

'Take a seat,' said Briony, removing a pile of paper from the only other chair. She leaned down and flicked on a kettle which was tucked away in a corner. 'Tell me about this event.'

'It's all a bit up in the air at the moment,' said Pippa. 'You see, Jeremy Lightfoot held a meeting about it in the village just the other week.'

'Jeremy Lightfoot, eh,' said Briony. She looked as if she could smell rotten eggs. 'Then why do you want to talk to me? I'm sure he's got more than enough celebrity chums who can come and lend a hand.'

'If it does come off,' said Pippa, 'I'll probably be organising it, and it would be nice to have different people —'

'Oh, and I'm different people?' said Briony. She seemed half-annoyed, half-amused.

'I don't mean that in a bad way,' said Pippa. 'I meant . . . less establishment.'

Briony frowned. 'So what made you come hunting for me?'

'Well, I found you on Twitter,' said Pippa, feeling as if Briony could see straight through her. 'And as you're local…'

'You mentioned Much Gadding,' said Briony. 'I take it you live there.' She paused. 'Have you met my Auntie Marge?'

Pippa wondered whether Briony would switch on her desk lamp and shine it in her face. 'Er, yes, I know Marge pretty well. But I didn't know about you until Daphne mentioned you.'

'Oh yes, Daphne.' Briony laughed, not a nice laugh. 'The guardian of the letters. Have you managed to get a peep at them?'

'I've seen one or two,' said Pippa.

'Typical,' said Briony. 'And I bet that . . . that twit Lightfoot has wangled himself open access.'

'No, he hasn't.' The kettle pinged, and Pippa breathed a sigh of relief as Briony's attention switched from her to coffee-making. She looked at Briony's profile; the prominent nose and chin, the firm mouth. Without the red hair, and the student clothes, Pippa suspected she would resemble Marge in forty years. *She's angry*, thought Pippa. *And she shoots from the hip. Hmm...* And as Briony was putting her mug of coffee on a nearby bookshelf, Pippa took her courage in both hands. 'You see, the letters have gone missing.'

Coffee slopped onto the coaster. 'Excuse me?' Briony hunted for a cloth. Finding none, she pulled a tissue from a box on the windowsill.

'They vanished after a meeting at Daphne's house,' said Pippa. 'Daphne doesn't want it to become a police matter, so I'm investigating.'

Briony goggled at her. 'But how come...?'

'Marge doesn't know,' said Pippa. 'Nobody knows at the moment apart from Daphne, me, and my husband, who isn't interested in the slightest.'

Briony puffed out a sigh. Then she laughed. 'Well, if I can't have them, they may as well disappear,' she said. 'Who do you think has stolen them?'

'There's more than one suspect,' Pippa said carefully.

Briony shot Pippa a look, then began to count on her fingers. 'Lightfoot, obviously—'

'Except that he's the one who asked me to persuade Daphne to share the letters,' said Pippa. 'He could have kept his mouth shut and got to work on them in peace and quiet.'

'I suppose,' said Briony, ungraciously. 'All right, who else?'

'Who is a friend of Daphne's,' said Pippa, keeping her voice steady, 'with a niece who could use a lucky break?'

Briony gasped. 'Auntie Marge would never—'

'No, I don't think she would either,' said Pippa. 'But I don't know.'

'So you want me to clear my auntie by helping you work out whodunnit?' said Briony. 'That's a very manipulative approach.'

'I actually came here to ask you what you knew about the poems and letters,' said Pippa. 'I didn't intend to take this line. It just sort of happened.'

'So emotional blackmail just sort of happens?' asked Briony, her already loud voice rising further.

'Marge has never mentioned you,' said Pippa. 'I only managed to track you down because you borrowed the library's *Selected Poems* before me, and the librarian remembered you.'

'I thought you said you were an event organiser,' said Briony, 'not a private eye.'

'I'm sort of both,' said Pippa.

'Interesting career choice,' commented Briony. 'So who hired you?'

'Daphne, I suppose,' said Pippa. 'But I'm also interested on my own behalf. I mean, I've read a few of the poems, and one of the letters, and if all the letters are like that, I don't see why anyone would want to steal them.'

Briony shrugged. 'Not that I've seen them, but probably the most interesting thing about those letters is that someone has stolen them. The ones in the *Selected Poems* are mostly predictable waffling about the Muse.' She drank her coffee reflectively. 'The other mystery is how Clementina Stoate, after several years of dull, worthy poetry, produced a few interesting poems, then one that was downright odd, and then stopped writing altogether. It's almost as if she ran out of ideas.'

'And that's what you'd like to investigate?' asked Pippa.

'Oh, there are plenty of things I'd like to investigate,' said Briony. 'Such as why, with a huge teaching load and a good number of publications in respectable journals, I'm still stuck on six-month contracts.'

'I'm afraid that's out of my remit,' said Pippa. 'But if there's a way you can help me find those letters, perhaps I can help you to get a proper look at them. Not to mention a speaking gig at the event.'

'So there is an event?' said Briony. 'You didn't make that up to get your foot in the door?'

'Of course not,' said Pippa indignantly.

A light tap sounded on the door. 'Come in,' called Briony.

A woman who clearly wasn't a student put her head round the door. 'Sorry to disturb you, Briony, but Professor Hartshorn wondered if he might have a quick word. It's about the marking for the eighteenth-century course, since Dr Jacobs has been signed off sick for the next three weeks.'

Briony sighed. 'And I suppose he wants that word right now?'

The woman looked apologetic. 'If you could…'

'Tell him I'll be along in five minutes, Naomi.' Briony drained her coffee cup and set it on the table. 'More work.' She scrutinised Pippa. 'That turned out quite interesting.'

'It did, rather,' said Pippa. 'I'll let you chew it over. But I must ask you not to tell Marge. Daphne was very clear on that.'

Briony frowned. 'All right,' she said. 'I won't tell her for now. But I don't like it.'

'I don't, either,' said Pippa. 'But Daphne is only trying to protect her. She's worried that she'll worry.'

'Daphne worries about everything, according to Auntie Marge,' said Briony. 'I'll be in touch. And no sneaky arresting my auntie, or you'll have me to deal with.'

'I won't be arresting anyone,' said Pippa, gathering her things.

Briony saw her out of the office, locked the door, and strode off, saying, 'You can see me at one o'clock, you know,' to the trio of hopeful students who were waiting outside the door.

Chapter 9

Pippa sighed and drew a line through Lady Higginbotham's name in her notepad. So far, interviewing wasn't going particularly well.

She had begun with Daphne on Friday evening, since they *were* her letters, and at least they could talk frankly without skating around the matter. Or at least, that was what Pippa had hoped. As it turned out, Daphne was hopelessly vague. She couldn't remember who had gone where, or when, whether anyone had shown a particular interest in the letters apart from Jeremy Lightfoot, or whether anyone had had a bag with them capable of accommodating the file. In addition, Daphne agreed enthusiastically with any opinion that Pippa advanced, until Pippa felt that everything she said was leading the witness. 'I think we can leave it there,' she said, closing her notepad.

'Was I any help, dear?' asked Daphne. 'I did try hard to remember, but it's all a bit of a jumble. It was such a busy evening, you see—'

'It was,' said Pippa.

'I don't see how we'll ever work out where those letters went,' said Daphne.

She looked defeated already. 'Well, I shall do my best to find them,' said Pippa.

'Thank you so much, dear,' said Daphne, and patted her arm.

Now it was Monday, and Pippa had taken the opportunity of Ruby's morning at Little Puffins to go to Higginbotham Hall, on the pretext of discussing costings for the Summer Proms.

Beryl Harbottle, Lady Higginbotham's housekeeper, appeared harried when she opened the door.

'Good morning, Beryl,' said Pippa. 'Everything all right?'

'Don't mention the literary festival,' said Beryl. 'She's been talking about it for most of the weekend. When I served breakfast, she asked me whether I thought Fiona Bruce or Kirsty Wark would be better to present the televised coverage.'

'I see,' said Pippa, grinning inwardly. In that case, it should be easy to divert Lady Higginbotham to the festival, and the evening at Daphne's house, without too much difficulty. 'Is Lady H in the morning room?'

'She is,' said Beryl. 'Researching publishers.'

Lady Higginbotham glanced up at Pippa's entrance, and smiled broadly. 'Do take a seat, Pippa. Would you like some tea?'

'I'd love some,' said Pippa. 'I just wanted to run costings for the proms past you, and go through the provisional bookings.' She felt she ought to make at least a pretence of getting down to business.

Within three minutes Lady Higginbotham had segued seamlessly from marquees for the proms to whether it would be better to hold the literary festival indoors or outdoors. 'It would probably be easier to film or record indoors, wouldn't it?' She looked thoughtful. 'Although they seem to manage on the Antiques Roadshow.'

'Don't forget it will only be a small event, Lady Higginbotham,' said Pippa. 'That is, if it happens at all.'

'Oh, but surely it will,' said Lady Higginbotham. 'I mean, Jeremy was so enthusiastic about those old letters at Clementina Stoate's house. And—' She looked bashful.

'And what?' asked Pippa.

'And he phoned me last week for a chat. He is very keen.'

'Jeremy *phoned* you?'

'Yes,' said Lady Higginbotham. 'I mean, the phone number for the Hall is on our website. It isn't hard to find.'

'No, I don't suppose it is,' said Pippa. 'Did you read any of the letters, Lady Higginbotham? I wondered what you thought of them.'

'No,' said Lady Higginbotham vaguely. 'I just listened when Jeremy read that one out. He does have a wonderful speaking voice, don't you think?'

'Um, yes,' said Pippa, not having thought about it.

'I'm sure it will be a great success,' said Lady Higginbotham firmly. 'And I shall do whatever I can to help. As far as I'm concerned, the Hall is at his disposal.'

'Mmm,' said Pippa, not reassured at all. 'It's a shame

that he couldn't borrow the letters, really, and start working on them.'

'Yes, it is,' said Lady Higginbotham. 'Documents such as those ought to be in the public domain. Or at least in a collection, or a museum, where they could be cared for properly. Not put away in plastic wallets in a tatty old ring binder.' Her eyes became unfocused as she pondered. 'Perhaps,' she said, 'they could be reproduced, and we could put the copies in frames on the wall of the Long Room. Like a gallery.'

'That's a lovely idea,' said Pippa. 'I know what I meant to ask you. I was admiring your outfit that evening, and particularly your handbag. Could you tell me what make it is? It's probably out of my price range, but—'

Lady Higginbotham looked simultaneously flattered and embarrassed. 'Oh, I'm not sure,' she said. 'I'll go and see if I can find it. Do excuse me a moment.' She got up, and scuttled from the room.

Left alone, Pippa tried the drawers of the desk. They were unlocked, and there was no telltale black file within, nor any letters. She crossed to the bookshelf, and inspected the volumes. All but one were too small to accommodate a plastic wallet without folding it, and Pippa had a strong feeling that Lady Higginbotham's reverence for Jeremy Lightfoot, if not the letters themselves, would keep her from manhandling the letters in any way. She pulled out the book – an illustrated atlas – and flicked through it, finding nothing. She heard footsteps, and hastily slid the book back on the shelf.

'Here it is,' said Lady Higginbotham, holding up a

smart navy bag. 'It's a Hermès Birkin bag. It was a present for my twenty-first.'

'It's beautiful,' said Pippa. 'And completely out of my price range, unfortunately.' Now the bag was in front of her, she did remember it. And it was clearly too small to hold a ring binder.

'Perhaps you could ask for one for a special birthday,' said Lady Higginbotham.

'Maybe I could,' said Pippa, imagining Simon's face if she did. 'That will give my husband a few years to save up.'

'I do like a nice handbag,' said Lady Higginbotham, very seriously, giving the bag a pat and setting it on a cushion as if it were a favourite dog. 'Now, where were we?'

Pippa let Lady Higginbotham take the lead for twenty minutes or so, taking occasional notes when she suggested something for the literary festival that might actually work. 'Well, that's been very useful, Lady Higginbotham,' she said. 'I've made a few notes, and perhaps we can start making arrangements when Jeremy Lightfoot gives us the all-clear.'

'Oh yes,' breathed Lady Higginbotham. 'It's so important to be prepared, don't you think?'

Sitting in the Mini, Pippa read the list of names in her notepad and debated who to try next. Then she consulted her watch. With less than an hour until pick-up time, the obvious next candidate was Norm.

As usual, Norm was at ease in the library, reading a thriller from his stock. This time it was Michael Crichton.

'Keeping busy, I see,' said Pippa.

'Making hay while the sun shines,' replied Norm, reaching for his bookmark. 'Have you come to pick up more crime books, in the absence of anything real-life to get your teeth into?'

Pippa looked at him; but Norm appeared completely guileless. *Then again*, she thought, *he used to be a policeman. He ought to be good at a poker face.* 'Actually,' she said, 'I wondered whether that copy of Clementina Stoate's poems had come back in yet.'

'Oh, that.' Norm got up, went to a shelf which Pippa had never looked at, and pulled out a familiar slim red volume, which he put into Pippa's hand. 'You're welcome to it,' he said.

'Have you read some, then?' asked Pippa.

Norm's stance seemed stiffer than usual. 'I was the borrower,' he said. 'I wanted to know what all the fuss was about.'

'I see,' said Pippa. 'I take it you didn't enjoy them?'

Norm made a face. 'What I find, Pippa, is that it rarely works if you open a book out of a sense of duty. I was invited to the meeting by that Jeremy Lightfoot chap, so I thought I should at least learn a bit more.' His mouth twisted into a wry smile. 'I suspected I might not enjoy it, and I was right. Lots of hearts and flowers stuff, full of classical references I should probably know and don't. A few towards the end were bearable, but I must admit I was glad when I finished.'

'You probably got further than most people,' said Pippa. She had dipped into the library book over the weekend, and her assessment was not dissimilar from Norm's. 'We have to think that those were different times.'

'That's as may be,' said Norm darkly. 'And I daresay that stuff was popular at the time. But I reckon Jeremy Lightfoot's got an uphill struggle persuading a modern audience to listen to that claptrap. To be honest, I went to that meeting out of politeness. As a member of the community, I thought I should take an interest in potential developments.'

'Oh yes,' said Pippa, 'I meant to ask. Did you get home in time for *Line of Duty*?'

'Oh yes,' said Norm. 'Only just, though.'

Pippa browsed through the book of poetry, thinking. She visualised Norm as he had left, hands stuck in pockets, whistling. *There's absolutely no reason for him to take the letters*, she thought. What on earth would he do with them? *If he were interested in old books and manuscripts, he wouldn't spend his days in here.*

'Can I take this?' she said. 'I doubt I'll enjoy it, but I suppose I ought to read them.' *And*, she thought, *hide the fact that I went all the way to Gadcester for a copy.*

'Fill your boots,' said Norm, and opened the ledger.

Pippa mentally crossed Norm off her list as she left the library, and checked her watch. Another fifteen minutes before she needed to get Ruby. The green was quiet, since the shops were closed, and it looked inviting on the bright spring day. *I shall sit and think for a few minutes.*

She had just sat down when her phone rang. *Much Gadding Police*, said the display. She had changed it when Jim Horsley left.

Pippa grimaced, and pressed *Answer*. 'Hello, Pippa Parker speaking,' she said.

'Good morning, Mrs Parker.' Pippa recognised PC Gannet's voice and her heart sank. 'I'd like a word, if I may.'

'Of course,' said Pippa automatically, bracing herself. 'I have to pick my daughter up in a few minutes, though, so if you want an extended conversation—'

'I ran into Miss Fairhurst this morning,' said PC Gannet, 'while I was on my beat around the village, and she almost fainted when she saw me.'

'I'm sorry,' said Pippa, 'but I don't understand what this has to do with me. I don't know any Miss Fairhurst.'

'Miss Daphne Fairhurst?'

Pippa said nothing.

'I take it that means you do know who I'm referring to,' said PC Gannet, in his best accusatory tone.

'I've met Daphne a couple of times—'

'She appears to know you *very* well,' said PC Gannet. 'I merely wished her good morning and she backed away from me, saying that she didn't know who had sent me, but that Pippa had it all under control and there was no need for my services. Before I could ask any more questions, the sus – the lady returned to her own house at a brisk pace, and closed the door behind her. I debated knocking and asking what on earth she was talking about, but then I decided the best thing to do was to go to the horse's mouth.' He paused. 'Since you have it all under control.'

'She might mean some other Pippa,' said Pippa.

PC Gannet let the sentence hang in the air for a bit. 'I

don't think so,' he said. 'So when you have some child-free time I would like you to report to Much Gadding Police Station at your earliest convenience, and explain what you're meddling in this time.'

Chapter 10

On Tuesday morning, Pippa knocked at the door of the police station with trepidation. Then she tried the handle, but the door didn't move. 'So much for accessibility,' she muttered.

After about a minute she heard footsteps, and the drawing of a bolt. The door opened a little, and PC Gannet regarded her sternly. 'You'd better come in, Mrs Parker,' he said. 'I'm finishing some paperwork.'

Pippa considered taking a seat, but decided that would probably lead to more delay. PC Gannet retreated behind the counter, picked up a pen, and wrote on something just out of Pippa's range of vision. She craned her neck, and saw that he was doing a sudoku puzzle.

'It's probably a nine,' she said. 'Look, I've got someone minding my two-year-old at playgroup. I really don't have time to wait.'

PC Gannet frowned, then stalked to the door and re-bolted it. 'We'd better go into the back room,' he said.

When she entered the back room Pippa noticed that the

film posters which had previously decorated the walls had been replaced by public information ones. 'Sit down,' said PC Gannet. 'What's going on, Mrs Parker?'

'Nothing,' said Pippa. 'Aren't you going to offer me tea?'

'Thought you were in a hurry,' said PC Gannet.

One all, thought Pippa.

PC Gannet took a seat opposite Pippa, and switched on the tape recorder. 'Interview with Mrs Pippa Parker, on the —'

'There's no need for that,' said Pippa. 'I already told you that this isn't a police matter.' She reached over and switched off the recorder.

PC Gannet glared at her. 'I'll decide whether it's a police matter or not.'

'Fine, I'll tell you,' said Pippa. 'And when I do, you'll agree that this really isn't anything to bother the police with. Apart from anything else, Daphne doesn't want you involved, so she won't report it. Therefore it *can't* be a police matter.'

PC Gannet looked mutinous. 'What can't?'

Pippa sighed. 'A folder full of old letters has gone missing, and I'm helping Daphne work out what's happened to them. That's it.'

A strange bark issued from PC Gannet, and Pippa realised it must be a laugh. 'Is that all it is? A load of old letters?'

'Yep,' said Pippa.

PC Gannet's shoulders went up and down silently. 'So why was she so freaked out when I met her in the village?'

Pippa leaned forward. 'To be honest, I think she's one of those conscientious old ladies who automatically feels guilty when she sees a policeman, even though she hasn't done anything, or when she goes through the green channel at customs, even though she's got nothing to declare.'

PC Gannet considered this. 'Oh,' he said. 'Is this another one of your psychological moment thingies?'

'Maybe it's related,' said Pippa.

'Mmm.' PC Gannet sat back in his chair and looked wise. 'Well, given what you've told me, I really don't think this is a police matter. Please don't come and bother me with things like this, Mrs Parker. I am a busy man, you know.'

Pippa snorted. 'I can see that.' She stood up. 'Never mind, PC Gannet, today's edition of the *Much Gadding Messenger* has a puzzle section. If you hurry, the country store might still have one.'

PC Gannet escorted her to the front door, and let her out. She noted that he didn't bolt it again, but stood in the doorway, watching her leave. Once she was out of view, Pippa stopped and waited. Sure enough, out shot PC Gannet, heading for the village green.

Poor man, thought Pippa. *He probably thought he was going to be a local hero, and instead he's rescuing cats and frightening pensioners.* Shaking her head, she returned to the playgroup.

Caitlin, whom Pippa had asked to mind Ruby, appeared to be taking life easy. 'She's over there,' she said, pointing.

Pippa followed her finger and spotted Ruby sitting in

the middle of the rug, bashing a rattle on the ground. 'Oh for heaven's sake,' she said. 'How long has she been doing that?'

Caitlin thought. 'She started not long after you left,' she said. 'I did ask her if she wanted a more grown-up toy, but she wouldn't have it. She said she wasn't allowed rattles in Cygnets, so she'd play with them here.'

'Ah,' said Pippa.

Caitlin gave her a sympathetic look. 'How's the big move going?'

'Not well,' said Pippa. 'When I collected her yesterday they said she'd had a tantrum. A proper rolling-on-the-floor screaming-her-head-off tantrum. That isn't like Ruby.'

'No, it isn't,' said Caitlin. 'She's always seemed rather grown-up. Certainly compared to my two.' She got up. 'Tea?'

'Yes please,' said Pippa. 'I've just had dealings with Gannet of the Yard.'

'Fun morning, then,' replied Caitlin. 'I'll see if there are any biscuits. Watch Josh, will you. He's playing with the garage.'

'Will do,' said Pippa. 'Ruby!'

Ruby stopped mid-bash. 'Yes, Mummy?'

'Come and talk to me,' said Pippa.

Ruby considered her invitation. 'We can talk at home,' she said, and resumed bashing the rattle on the rug.

'Please stop doing that,' said Pippa. 'You'll break it. And a real baby might want that rattle.'

Ruby stuck her bottom lip out. Then she started to hiccup.

'No, Ruby, no…' Pippa scooped Ruby up as she began to wail, and carried her to her seat. Ruby buried her face in Pippa's top, and warm wet tears seeped through. Pippa sighed, and stroked Ruby's back. On balance, she preferred dealing with PC Gannet. He was easier to manipulate.

The poor lad must be so bored, she thought. *Even so, I need to get those letters found before he sticks his nose in. The last thing I need is PC Gannet putting his size tens where they're not wanted.*

Ruby let out a great big sniffly sigh, and Pippa kissed the top of her head. 'All better?' she asked.

'Can I play with the rattle?' Ruby asked in a small voice.

It was Pippa's turn to sigh. 'Yes, so long as you're careful with it. You don't want to break it, do you?'

Ruby shook her head. 'Nooooo.' Gripping the rattle, she slid off Pippa's lap, went back to the rug, and sat down. She picked up a board book and began turning the pages. When the rattle got in her way, she put it on the rug.

It's probably a phase, thought Pippa. *I really shouldn't worry. But I might give Sheila's a miss today. Just in case.*

'Here you go,' said Caitlin, handing her an institutional blue cup with a chocolate chip cookie in the saucer. 'I've pinched the last two. After this there's only Rich Tea.'

The biscuit in the saucer reminded Pippa of her visit to Daphne. Not that she needed reminding. Those stupid letters were taking over her life. She thought of her notepad, and the list of names. Marge and Malcolm were left.

'I may pop in and see Marge,' she said.

Caitlin looked blank. 'I'm sorry, who?'

'Oh, just a friend,' said Pippa. 'It would cheer Ruby up.'

'She's at a funny age,' said Caitlin. 'I'm thinking of getting lash extensions. What do you reckon?'

Pippa peered at Caitlin's eyelashes, which were thick and dark and needed no help at all. 'I reckon you're at a funny age,' she said.

***

After playgroup Pippa made Ruby her favourite lunch, then announced that they were going for a walk. 'And if Auntie Marge is in, we might visit,' she said.

Ruby jumped up and down. 'Auntie Marge! Auntie Marge!' Then she grinned. 'Freddie will be cross. He likes Auntie Marge.'

'That's what you get for going to school,' said Pippa, pushing aside thoughts of the work she ought to be doing. *When the kids are in bed, maybe.*

Ruby practically pulled her out of the house, into the village, and along River Lane. 'Can we visit Sippidippy?'

'Serendipity won't be in,' said Pippa. 'She's away on a book tour.'

'A book tour?' asked Ruby. 'What's that?'

'Well,' said Pippa, 'when you write a book, sometimes you get invited to go and talk about it at bookshops and libraries and places like that. You tell people about your book so that they will buy a copy.'

Ruby nodded wisely. 'Can I write a book?'

'I don't see why not,' said Pippa. 'But you might need to learn to read and write first.'

'I can write,' said Ruby importantly. 'I wrote a very good A. Rach said. In Cygnets.'

'That's certainly a start,' said Pippa. 'You can write an A for me later, if you like. Now let's see if Auntie Marge is in.'

She knocked at the door, and a minute later it began to open. Beyoncé shot between Ruby's legs, ran up the nearest tree, then sat washing her whiskers.

'Oh, it's you,' said Marge, looking a tiny bit disappointed.

'Yes,' said Pippa. 'I was passing, and it occurred to me that I hadn't popped in for a while.'

'Passing, eh?' said Marge. 'Were you on your way to swim in the river?'

'You know what I mean,' said Pippa. 'Ruby just told me that she can write the letter A.'

'Well, now,' said Marge. 'You'd better show me, young Ruby.'

Ruby squeezed through the small gap between Marge and the door. 'I need paper and crayons,' she said.

'I'll see what I can do,' said Marge. 'Come on in, Pippa.'

Marge's front room was in its usual comfortable disarray. 'Excuse the mess,' said Marge. 'I was on a bit of a Fortnite marathon. Cuppa?'

'You know I never refuse tea,' said Pippa.

'Good point. I'll find supplies for Ruby, then I'll get on the case.'

Pippa shot a glance at her, but Marge's face showed no sign of suspicion. 'Lovely,' she said, and sat down. Marge went off with Ruby, muttering about crayons, and presently Pippa heard her clattering in the galley kitchen.

She got up, and tiptoed towards the shelves. They were the kind with a small cupboard underneath, and a wide drawer in the middle. Pippa opened the doors gently, and was confronted by piles of computer games. No file here, she thought, and closed the cupboard. Next she tried to open the drawer, but it wouldn't budge more than a centimetre or so. Was that because it hadn't been opened in a long time, or because something inside was making it stick? Pippa jiggled the drawer handles, to no avail. Then she peered in, but could see nothing. She heard footsteps, and hastily pushed the drawer closed.

'Right,' said Marge, 'paper and crayons for Ruby, and tea for us.' She set down a mug which said *Gamer For Life* on the coaster nearest Pippa. 'I thought you'd come for a post-mortem.'

'Excuse me?' said Pippa.

'You know,' said Marge. 'After that meeting with Mr Jeremy Light-Fingers.'

Pippa goggled. 'What do you mean?'

'Oh come on,' said Marge. 'Anyone could see that he wanted to cart off as much of Daphne's stuff as he possibly could.'

Pippa watched Ruby, kneeling up to the coffee table, tongue stuck out in concentration while she drew a blue circle. 'Yes, but he didn't, did he?'

'Not for want of trying,' said Marge darkly. 'That's exactly what I was afraid of.'

Pippa tried to think of a suitable response. Was Marge

diverting attention from herself? Or attempting to heap suspicion on Jeremy Lightfoot even before it was common knowledge that the letters had gone missing? 'I'm sure Daphne's fine,' she said lamely.

'I'm not,' said Marge. 'I haven't seen her since that evening, you know. I've rung a couple of times, but she keeps saying that she's too busy to talk.' She leaned forward and lowered her voice. 'I'm a bit worried about her. I think she's feeling the strain.'

'I think you're right,' said Pippa. Marge wore the expression of a concerned friend. *I hate this*, she thought. *I hate suspecting my friends.* 'What do you think we should do?'

Marge gave Pippa a very direct look, and Pippa was reminded of Briony. 'You should turn down the literary festival, and put Lady Higginbotham off the idea,' she said. 'Easier said than done, I know, but it's the only chance for Daphne to have some peace and quiet.'

'Look, Mummy! Look, Auntie Marge!' Ruby held up her paper. 'I wrote an A!'

Pippa inspected the paper, on which, indeed, was a wobbly but recognisable lower-case a. 'Well done, Ruby,' she said. 'That's a very good A.'

'It is,' Marge agreed.

Ruby beamed. 'Can I write my book now?'

Marge huffed. 'If I were you, Ruby, I'd stay clear of writing books. They lead to trouble.'

Ruby pouted. 'Wanna do book tour!'

Marge stared. 'Of course you do,' she said eventually.

Ruby wrote three more As while Pippa finished her tea.

'I think you're ready for B,' said Pippa, 'but I'll demonstrate that at home.'

'I shall look forward to seeing that,' said Marge. 'In the meantime, remember what I said, Pippa.' She mouthed, *'No festival.'*

'I'll bear it in mind,' said Pippa. 'But it isn't down to me.'

'I wish it were,' said Marge, as she saw them to the door. 'Don't be a stranger.'

Marge was still waving when Pippa and Ruby turned onto the main part of River Lane. *She's missing her friend*, thought Pippa, and felt a pang of guilt that she couldn't be honest with Marge. *But is she being honest with me?* She shook her head to get rid of the thought. *I wish . . . what do I wish?* She wasn't sure. *Not this, at any rate. This is not the sort of new thing I had in mind.*

'Can we do B?' asked Ruby.

'Yes, of course we can,' said Pippa. 'We might even get as far as C before we have to fetch Freddie.'

'C?' And Ruby dragged Pippa all the way home, so keen was she to begin her literary career.

Chapter 11

'So, are you going tonight?' said Lila.

Pippa stared at her while the children snaked into the classroom. 'Going where?'

Lila stared back. 'To Jeff's gig? At Rumours?'

Comprehension dawned. 'Oh heck, I'd forgotten it was tonight.'

Lila rolled her eyes. 'Well, I'm going. My sister is babysitting Bella. She wanted to come, but I don't think Rumours is any place for a five-year-old.' She looked at Pippa. 'I take it that means you aren't coming.'

Pippa thought. 'I could... I could ask Simon to deal with the kids.' She eyed Lila. 'What time does it start?'

Lila tutted. 'Their set begins at eight, they're doing an hour, and depending on how it's going they might do another hour after the break.'

'Oh, OK,' said Pippa. 'Maybe I could come for the first hour, then.'

Lila studied her. 'I thought you'd want to meet Jed James,' she said. 'Cultivate him as a contact. That sort of thing.'

'If I was in the habit of promoting bands, I probably would,' said Pippa.

Lila looked rather hurt.

'Sorry,' said Pippa, 'I'm a bit on edge. Things have got very busy lately.' *And I was planning to go to choir tonight*, she thought, with regret.

'If you can't make it, you can't,' said Lila. 'But it would've been nice to get out together. Wear something other than jeans and joggers, do something other than the school run and work.'

'Mmm,' said Pippa. *At the moment, doing just the school run and work would suit me fine.* 'I'd better go,' she said. 'Time to drop Ruby at nursery.' *For a full day*, she thought, and tried not to shiver. 'Have you talked to Jeff about – you know what?' she said, to take her mind off it.

'I'm getting round to it,' said Lila. 'You can't rush these things.'

Pippa had decided to take Ruby to nursery after the school run today, so that she could have a chat with Rach. But as they walked towards the nursery she noticed that Ruby's feet were dragging, and she was getting slower and slower. 'Come along,' she said, 'or we'll never get there.'

Ruby said nothing.

Pippa stopped and looked down at her. 'It won't be so bad,' she said. 'I know it takes some getting used to, moving into a new room—'

'Everyone's big there!' Ruby wailed. 'They can do lots of things! And I can't!'

'Oh dear.' Pippa thought about picking Ruby up and

giving her a cuddle, but that didn't seem appropriate, somehow. 'Let's go and sit on the green for a couple of minutes,' she said.

'I don't have to go?' Ruby asked, her face lighting up.

Pippa didn't answer until they were both sitting on a bench. A duck approached then, seeing that they had no food, waddled away with a quack of disgust. 'The thing is, Ruby, at some point you *will* go into the Cygnets. You've moved up *because* you can do everything in Ducklings. And when those bigger children went into Cygnets, I bet they couldn't do all the things either.'

Ruby's eyes opened wide. 'Really?'

'Yes, really,' said Pippa. 'And that's why they went into the Cygnet Room, to learn how.'

'Ohhh,' said Ruby, with an air of great understanding.

'And one day,' said Pippa, 'you'll be one of the big children in that room, and there will be little ones like you coming in. But I'm sure that you'll help them, because you'll know what it was like to be a small person in a big room.'

'Can we go now?' said Ruby. 'I want to learn things and be big.'

I hope it sticks, thought Pippa.

Ruby ran into the room quite willingly, and Pippa beckoned Rach over for a chat. 'I've been talking to Ruby this morning, and she seems OK,' she said. 'But if it doesn't work out again, maybe she should go back to the other room.'

Rach nodded. 'I was going to say the same,' she said. 'What I might do is give her an hour in here this morning, move her into the smaller room for the rest of the morning, then bring her back in when the other room is full.'

'What a good idea,' said Pippa. She gave Ruby a goodbye cuddle, and went home feeling that perhaps things were manageable after all.

Then she got home, opened her laptop, and revised her opinion. The band she had wanted to open the Summer Proms had replied, saying that unfortunately they were committed on that day. The cheapest marquee quote turned out to be for a tent half the size she needed. And Jed James had emailed with a list of dos and don'ts for the gig tonight. Then, to top it off, her phone buzzed.

Lady H: *Have you been able to put together those quotes yet, Pippa? I don't want to press you, but time is of the essence.*

Ping! And another email landed in her inbox, headed *Reminder*. Pippa saw the name Jeremy Lightfoot and slammed the lid of her laptop down. *I need a drink*, she thought. *A stiff drink for preference, but I suppose it had better be tea.*

As Pippa reached into the cupboard for a mug, she noticed her hand was shaking. *This is ridiculous*, she thought. *I can't go on like this.* She leaned on the worktop, ran her hands through her hair, and took several deep breaths. *I should probably start meditating.*

She stayed there until the kettle boiled. The sound of water pouring into the mug calmed her. *Very Zen.* She made her tea, took it back into the dining room, set it down, then pushed her laptop out of reach and opened her notepad.

What can I not do? she wrote, and underlined it.

I don't have to go to Rumours tonight.
I don't have to go to choir tonight (although I'd like to).
I don't have to be involved in the literary festival.
I don't have to do this investigation.

Pippa contemplated what she had written, then picked up her phone. Her first text was to Lila. *I'd like to come to Rumours tonight, but I'm exhausted*, she typed. *Can you let me know how it goes? I'm sure you can schmooze Jed James for me x*

She felt lighter already. *I'll see how I feel about choir later.*

Pippa took a deep breath, opened Lady Higginbotham's text, and pressed *Reply*. *I'm not sure I have capacity to organise a literary festival on top of everything else*, she wrote. *And I don't think it's worth doing quotes till we have an idea of what Jeremy wants and how much he has to spend. Hope that's OK.*

Pippa looked at the last item on the list: the investigation. *Do I need to do anything there, apart from return the books?* Then she remembered Briony. *She's already so busy. I must let her know.*

She opened her laptop and scrolled quickly to Briony's last email. *It seemed such an adventure then*, she thought. Was it really less than a week since she had sat in Briony's cramped office? She sighed, and pressed the *Reply* button.

Dear Briony,

Sorry to spring this on you, after our discussion last week, but I don't have time to investigate the missing letters. My workload has increased recently, and I am also having childcare problems.

I hope you haven't spent much time on this matter, if any. I may still be involved in the literary festival if it goes ahead, and of course I shall recommend you as a potential speaker. I'm sure that you will do a great job.

Kind regards, and apologies again,
Pippa Parker

She read the email through quickly, then pressed *Send* before she could change her mind. Then she switched to the Short Back and Sides inbox, re-read Jed James's email, and composed a reply questioning most of his conditions. *Don't you push my client around*, she thought, as she typed furiously.

Pippa lost herself in routine tasks until her stomach rumbled at a quarter to two. She looked at the time in disbelief. *Of course, I haven't had to fetch Ruby.* She felt a pang of guilt that she had forgotten her daughter, then relieved that the nursery hadn't phoned her. Presumably everything was all right. *And if it isn't*, thought Pippa, *I can always drop the Wednesday afternoon session, and fit in Jeff's work somewhere else.* She closed the laptop, turned up the volume on the radio, and decided to treat herself to cheese on toast, eaten with both hands, and without constant diversions from Ruby.

As she was popping the last corner in her mouth, her

phone rang. The display said *Unknown Number*. Pippa was about to press *Refuse* when a thought stopped her. *What if it's Jed James with something important for tonight?* She sighed, and took the call.

'Hello Pippa,' said a loud, definite voice she recognised immediately. 'It's Briony Shepherd. I hope it isn't a bad time.'

'No, it's fine,' said Pippa. 'How did you get my number?'

'I'd like to tell you that I tracked it down through my expert detective skills,' said Briony. 'But it's in your email signature.'

'Oh,' said Pippa.

'Anyway,' said Briony, 'I got your email. Why the change of heart?'

'I'm just busy,' said Pippa.

'But you were all fired up when we met,' said Briony.

'I was,' said Pippa. 'But life has a habit of getting in the way. And it's awful investigating when your friends are involved.'

There was a brief silence. 'It must be,' said Briony. 'But I've been doing a bit of digging, and I think you should keep going.'

'You're the only one, then,' said Pippa. 'Daphne's quite relieved not to have the responsibility of the letters any more.'

'Oh, stuff Daphne,' said Briony. 'If people stopped doing things because other people wanted them to, what would happen?'

'I'd have a lot more spare time,' said Pippa. 'And a lot

less guilt.'

'I've been rereading the letters and the poems,' said Briony.

'How?' asked Pippa. 'I've got the Gadcester library copy.'

'Don't tell anyone,' said Briony, 'but I photocopied it. I've spent some time reading the letters Clementina wrote around the time when her most famous poems got published, and it was kind of interesting.'

'I'm glad you enjoyed it,' said Pippa, 'but it's nothing to do with me any more.'

'Yes it is,' said Briony. 'You told me that you investigate things. Well, investigate this. Go and read the good poems – you know which ones – then read the letters written up to a year before, and tell me what you find. I want to check it isn't just me.'

'What isn't just you?' cried Pippa.

'You'll see when you read them,' said Briony. 'Must go, I've got a class in two minutes. Bye, Pippa.' And the phone went dead.

Pippa stared at the phone, then laid it gently on the table. *I tried to pull myself out of one mystery, and I've had another one dropped in my lap. Oh well, half an hour's reading can't hurt.* She turned to a new page on her notepad, fetched the *Selected Poems*, and set to work.

Chapter 12

Pippa frowned and reread the letter.

14th April
Dear Mr Chapman,
Thank you very much for your letter, and for your kind remarks on the two poems, 'Daisies at Dawn' and 'The Rabbit', which I sent you. I am so glad that you enjoyed them, and look forward to seeing them in the magazine in due course.

At this point I should reveal that the name under which I sent the poems, Miss M. Wright, is in fact a pseudonym. My name is Mrs Clementina Stoate, and I have published several poems before, but not in this style. I wanted to use a false name so that my work would not be pre-judged. I hope you will forgive my small deception.

Yours sincerely,
Clementina Stoate

Pippa turned to the poems. 'Daisies at Dawn' and 'The

105

Rabbit' were both there, and she read them through. They were short, simple, and powerful. For comparison, she flicked back to the first poem in the selection, called 'To My Muse'.

O much-esteemed Euterpe, vouchsafe me
But one leaf from your laurel, or the breath
Which sings through Pan's sweet pipes, for poetry
Enduring through the ages, thwarting death—

'Ugh,' murmured Pippa, and returned to the letters. The letter before the one to Mr Chapman was written to her friend Phoebe, and seemed much more cheerful than the missive which Jeremy Lightfoot had read aloud.

10th April
Dear Phoebe,
Many thanks for your letter. I am well, and Charles is not unwell, which is perhaps the best that can be said.
Perhaps it is the coming of spring, but I find myself in great spirits. It must be the influence of nature. I am taking a walk every day, or at the very least sitting in my garden, and it has inspired me. I am experimenting with new forms. I cannot say whether the result is good or not; I am just letting the Muse lead me where she will.
Thank you for your enquiry about my maid. I know I could engage a new one, and get rid of her, for it is true that Mary is a sorry excuse for a maid. I could no doubt engage a better one if I walked into the street and hailed the first young woman that I saw. However, I suppose we

have got used to each other. At any rate, she does not annoy me quite as much as she used to. Perhaps I am growing more tolerant.

Do tell me when you could come and visit. The village is looking at its best now, and while I know it is a long journey, with this fine weather the roads will not be better this year.

With love,
Clementina

'Inspired by spring, eh,' murmured Pippa. She turned back to 'Daisies at Dawn' and read the poem preceding it, 'Meditation on a Roman Head', which resembled the one about Clementina's muse. It was dated a full year earlier. *Then again,* she thought, *how many poems did she write which aren't included?*

The volume had a short introduction, which she skimmed. *Clementina Stoate was a minor poetic talent of the Victorian age,* she read.

Pippa raised her eyebrows. 'Charming.'

However, among the many rather worthy poems which appear in periodicals of the time, she contributed a handful of quite remarkable ones. Hers was a late flowering and a short one, for she enjoyed barely two years of this creative inspiration before her poetic well, seemingly, ran dry. This coincided with the death of her husband, Charles.

As it turned out, Clementina Stoate did not outlive her husband by many years. After his death she shunned the limelight, and died alone in the house where she had spent her adult life, nestled in a sleepy village in Gadcestershire.

'He could at least have given Much Gadding a mention,' murmured Pippa.

Mrs Stoate's last poem, 'The Key', has baffled all attempts to interpret it. In some ways it is an unwelcome return to the vague and mystical style of her earlier work, but it is driven by an emotion more akin to that shown in her later anthologised poems.

Pippa turned to 'The Key', read the first few lines, and decided it was beyond her, too. Then she closed the book.

She recalled her conversation with Briony. *I've done what she asked me to*, she thought. *Do I agree?* But Briony had been very cagey as to what she actually thought.

Pippa could feel a headache developing, and rubbed her hands over her face to push it away. Then she got up and looked out at the garden, in the hope that nature might inspire her in the same way as it had worked its magic on Clementina Stoate.

Something isn't right. I don't know what it is, but—

She picked up a pen. *Clementina Stoate changed the style of her poetry completely in 1878*, she wrote. *She also sent poems to a different magazine. Why?*

She stared at that for a while, then wrote again. *She stopped writing when her husband died, but he wasn't the source of inspiration for her poems. Perhaps she was grief-stricken, though, and never recovered.*

But something still isn't right, she thought. *If only – and I can't believe I'm thinking this – if only I could read all the poems, and all the letters. Maybe then Briony and I could make sense of it.*

Pippa reopened her laptop. The last email Briony had sent her was still highlighted, and she pressed *Reply*. *I did what you said, and you have a point*, she typed. *But I don't know what to do about it. Pippa.*

Briony's reply came swiftly. *Find the letters. I'll try and ring you later.*

I'm not sure I want you to, thought Pippa. *I don't think I can face yet more things to do.* She returned to the list she had made, headed *What can I not do*, and her mouth twisted. *I need advice.*

She looked at her phone as if it might bite her, then reached for it. She scrolled through the contacts until she found PC Horsley.

He might have changed his phone, she thought. *He might not have the same number. Or he could be in a meeting.* But the phone was already ringing.

'Hello, Pippa,' said Jim Horsley. He sounded exactly the same as usual.

'Hello, Jim. Is this a bad time to call?'

'Not particularly,' said Jim. 'I'm on my lunch break.'

'Oh,' said Pippa. 'Can you talk? I mean, I don't want to interrupt anything.'

'I'm eating a ham sandwich at my desk, Pippa,' said Jim. 'Now, what can I do for you? I assume that this isn't just a friendly catch-up call.'

Was it her imagination, or was there a note of

amusement in his voice? 'Could I talk to you off the record?'

'Oh heck,' said Jim. 'What have you done now?'

'I haven't done anything,' said Pippa. 'It isn't a police matter, and anyway, PC Gannet already knows about it.'

'Why does Gabe know about it if it isn't a police matter?' Jim sounded deeply suspicious.

'It's a long story,' said Pippa. 'Look, can I talk off the record or not?'

Jim sighed. 'I suppose. Go on, hit me.'

'It's to do with some old letters which have disappeared. The owner doesn't want any fuss, which includes police fuss, but obviously she'd like them back.'

'When you say disappeared,' said Jim, 'I presume you mean someone has taken them.'

'Well, yes,' said Pippa.

'OK, do you have an idea of who? A list of suspects?'

'Yes,' said Pippa, 'but that isn't all. The letters are written by a nineteenth-century poet.'

'So what do you want me to help with? I'm afraid I finished with poetry after GCSE English,' said Jim.

'Well, I've got this academic involved. She thinks there's something behind it all and wants me to help her work out what. But I'm so busy—'

'Then say no,' said Jim. 'It isn't your job, is it?'

'I know that,' said Pippa. 'But maybe these letters are much more important than we thought.'

'So does the owner really, really, want them back?'

Pippa sighed. 'To be honest, I'm not sure.'

'If she was that bothered, she'd ring the police,' said

Jim. 'So you needn't feel bad about not taking this on, if other things are more important.'

'But this is important too!' cried Pippa.

Jim laughed. 'And that's why you didn't need to phone me, Pippa; you'll do what you want anyway. I've worked on enough cases with you to know that if you're set on something, nothing gets in your way.'

'Am I so transparent?' said Pippa.

'To me, yes.' She could hear the smile in Jim's voice, and basked in the warmth.

'What's it like working in Gadcester?' she asked.

There was a pause before Jim answered. 'Oh, you know. Busy. Bigger cases. And I'm spending a lot more time with the inspector, so I'm learning. Which is good.'

'But…?'

'I suppose I miss being my own boss at Much Gadding,' said Jim. 'How's Gabe getting on?'

'Give him another month and he'll be a sudoku master,' said Pippa.

Jim snorted. 'I'd better go. Got to be somewhere in ten minutes.' A brief pause. 'It was nice talking to you, Pippa. Let me know how you get on. Off the record, of course.'

'Of course. Bye, Jim.' And Pippa ended the call. She smiled. Jim was probably right. It was an annoying habit of his. In fact… Her smile broadened. In fact, by telling him about the case, she had committed herself to taking it on. Once Jim knew, it was a matter of honour that she would solve it. 'I guess I'm in,' she said softly. 'But first, I'd better sort out what's happening at tonight's gig, or I'll be a client down before I know where I am.'

Pippa spent the rest of her afternoon dealing with pressing matters; but every so often she found herself looking at her notebook, and thinking: *I'll get back to you. It's only a matter of time.*

Chapter 13

'So, how did it go?' asked Pippa, flinching as two children not much smaller than her thundered past, missing her by centimetres.

Lila looked mutinous. 'Fine. Great, actually.' She smiled, a shy, proud smile. 'They did the first hour, then in the break Jed James asked if they could do another full hour. And he's asked them to do five more.'

'Wow,' said Pippa. She had meant to text Jeff after the gig, but hadn't been sure when it would end, or, if it hadn't gone well, how he would receive it. While puzzling over the matter, she'd fallen asleep, which settled it. 'And is Jeff happy?'

'Oh yes,' said Lila. 'Like a dog with two tails. I just worry—'

'It's only Gadcester,' said Pippa. 'It isn't as if he's going to the ends of the earth.'

'Yes, but what if someone spots him?' said Lila. 'Them, I mean. The group.'

'Exactly,' said Pippa. 'I doubt the whole group can

mobilise at a moment's notice. They've got jobs, haven't they?'

'I suppose,' said Lila, looking a little brighter.

'Why don't you enjoy it?' said Pippa. 'Jeff's got a new opportunity, he's happy, I assume the money suits him—'

'Oh yes,' said Lila. 'Although I have plans for that. After Bella, and – you know – I didn't think I'd be having any more kids, so I gave my baby stuff away. This could be a baby nest egg.'

'Have you mentioned that yet?' asked Pippa.

Lila raised her eyebrows. 'How could I? I've been focusing on Jeff's gig.'

'OK,' said Pippa. 'I'll get in touch with Jed James and get things formalised.'

The bell rang. 'At last,' said Lila. 'I thought when Bella went to school I'd stop getting the side-eye from work for coming in late. The teachers are way less punctual than I am.'

'If I had to deal with thirty kids, I doubt I'd come to work at all,' said Pippa.

'There is that,' admitted Lila, with a wry smile.

***

'Is it nursery?' asked Ruby, as they walked out of the school grounds.

'It's Thursday, Ruby,' said Pippa. 'Playgroup day.'

'Oh,' said Ruby, and her mouth turned down.

'You can go to Little Puffins tomorrow morning,' said Pippa. 'But I'm glad you like it better now.'

Pippa had received a glowing report from Rach when she arrived to pick Ruby up on Wednesday afternoon. 'No tears today,' said Rach, 'and no tantrums, and she played with two of the other children.'

'Excellent,' said Pippa.

Freddie looked around curiously. 'I don't remember this room,' he said.

'Of course you don't,' said Pippa. 'You went to the preschool, remember?'

'Oh yes,' said Freddie. 'That was ages ago.'

Pippa laughed. 'I suppose six months is a long time when you're only five.'

'Five is a *lot*,' said Freddie, drawing himself up to his full height and gazing round with a superior air.

Pippa snapped back to the present, and looked at the small girl trotting beside her. One day she would be as big as Freddie, and quite possibly being superior about having reached the grand old age of five. 'Now, Ruby, I have a couple of things to do before playgroup. If I put a DVD on, will you sit quietly and watch it? I'll bring my laptop in, and we can have quiet time together.'

Ruby considered the offer. 'Can I have squash?'

'Yes, if you're careful,' Pippa replied, considering this a small concession.

At home they settled down together, Pippa with her laptop and phone, and Ruby glued to a cartoon about fairies. Pippa disapproved of its girliness, but it was a useful tool in her armoury.

She worked quickly through some admin; an email to Jed James, two replies to bands who could be replacement openers for the Summer Proms, and checking out four new bookings for Lady Higginbotham's holiday lets.

Her next task was an email to Jeremy Lightfoot. *I have neglected him shamefully*, she thought. *Not with regard to the literary festival, but in his main role as chief suspect in the Case of the Missing Letters.*

She thought for a moment, then began to type.

Dear Jeremy,

I have had a chat to Daphne regarding your request about the letters. However, she is reluctant to release them.

If you could give Daphne a clear idea of what you intend to do with the letters, that would help your case. If you reply to this email with that information, I shall pass it on.

Hope all is well with you,
Pippa Parker

The reply came instantaneously, and was headed *Out Of Office*.

Dear Enquirer,

I am currently on study leave, and away from my desk. For any pressing matter, please contact the departmental admin team.

Yours in haste,
Jeremy Lightfoot

He's done a runner, thought Pippa. *He's got the letters, and he's working on them in a secret bunker somewhere. I've a good mind to—*

A good mind to what? Set the police on him? That was

exactly what Daphne didn't want. Apart from anything else, how could she track him down? Pippa had a feeling that the departmental admin team, even if they knew where he was, wouldn't divulge that information. She sighed. And she had absolutely no evidence beyond an obvious motive and a slim opportunity.

'Mummy, what's the time?' asked Ruby. 'I've watched three cartoons.'

Pippa checked her watch. 'Time to go to playgroup,' she said. 'In fact it was time to do that ten minutes ago. Sorry, I got caught up.'

'Oh, Mummy,' said Ruby, looking disappointed in her. 'People are waiting.' She paused the DVD, then slid off the sofa. 'Shoes on.'

Pippa followed in Ruby's wake, half-dazed. Could Jeremy Lightfoot really have pinched those letters from under their noses and made off with them? *He's got more front than Brighton*, she thought grimly. *He thinks he's on to something. And if I can stop him, I shall.* That matter resolved for now, she headed off to playgroup with a spring in her step.

***

'You're going round to Daphne's again?' said Simon. 'To do what? You said you hadn't made any progress.'

'Well,' said Pippa, 'I haven't made any progress in the normal sense of the word, but my understanding has grown.'

Simon looked at her doubtfully. 'Do you think she'll appreciate that if you go round and tell her?'

'No idea,' said Pippa. 'But I want to know more about

117

Clementina Stoate, and find out what else Daphne has stashed away. If anything.'

Simon sighed. 'How long do you think you'll be this time?'

'I don't know,' said Pippa. 'Probably not long. She might send me away with a flea in my ear.'

'How delightful,' said Simon. 'From what you said, though, she isn't that sort of person. She'll probably apologise to you because you haven't found her letters yet.'

Pippa giggled. 'I wouldn't be that surprised.' She eyed Simon. 'So does that mean you're happy to do bedtime?'

Simon rolled his eyes. 'Do I have a choice?' Then he gave Pippa a one-armed hug. 'It's nice to see you looking a bit less . . . overwhelmed.'

Pippa stared. 'Was I?'

'Yeah,' said Simon. 'You looked as if you had too much to do and you weren't enjoying any of it.'

Pippa grimaced. 'I'm sure that feeling will come back. Knowing my luck, sooner rather than later.'

'Be off with you, Little Miss Cheerful,' said Simon. 'You've got a case to work on.'

After encountering Jeremy Lightfoot's out of office, Pippa half-expected Daphne not to answer her door. But within a minute or so she heard the rattling of a door chain being taken off, and the door opened about an inch. 'Hello, Pippa,' said Daphne. 'I was just checking that you weren't the police. I didn't think you were tall enough to be young Constable Gannet.'

'No, I don't suppose I am,' said Pippa. 'May I come in?'

'Oh yes, yes,' said Daphne. She opened the door wide, admitted Pippa, then closed the door, locked it, and put the chain back on. 'You can't be too careful these days,' she said vaguely. 'Now.' She peered at Pippa. 'Do you have any news?'

'Not as such,' said Pippa. 'I've done some careful interviewing of people who were here that evening. Mostly, I've discounted them.' She didn't mention her continuing worry about Marge. 'I haven't managed to get hold of Malcolm, but I don't think he is the culprit, and I don't want to worry him. He's nervous, you see.'

'Oh yes, he is,' Daphne agreed, nodding fervently. 'And you're right. I don't see how it could be Malcolm. He didn't have a bag with him, or a big coat, or anything like that.'

'Excellent,' said Pippa. 'That's really helpful, Daphne. So we can rule him out.' She paused. 'The other person I haven't managed to get hold of is Jeremy Lightfoot. I emailed him earlier today, and I got a message that he was away on . . . *study leave.*'

'Oh,' said Daphne. She frowned.

'Yes, I know,' said Pippa. 'However, I can't go to the police with nothing more than suspicion.'

'Oh no, not the police,' said Daphne. 'I mean, that poor man—'

'If he did take your letters,' said Pippa, 'I think it's because he saw a letter that evening which interested him. He might be on to something. And I wonder whether we can work out what that is.'

'But how?' said Daphne.

Pippa studied Daphne, who was leaning forward and looking puzzled. 'Do you have any copies of the letters? I've been reading the selected poems and letters, and there's something I can't put my finger on, not without seeing more of Clementina Stoate's writing.' She paused. 'I hope you don't mind, but I talked to Marge's niece Briony. The one at the University of Gadcester.'

'Oh yes, Briony.' Daphne sighed. 'She's very . . . forthright.'

'She is,' said Pippa. 'But she also thinks that there's a mystery behind the letters and the poems, and she'd like to work out what it is too. So we were wondering... If Jeremy Lightfoot has taken the letters to do some sneaky research, you could help us thwart him by lending us anything you have which might help us get there first.'

'Oh,' said Daphne. 'I'm not sure about that. I mean, the letters—'

'The other thing,' said Pippa, improvising frantically, 'is that if you did let us borrow anything, and we solved the mystery before Jeremy Lightfoot, then the disappearance of the letters would never come out, and we wouldn't have to get the police involved. I know you don't want that.'

'Oh, I see,' said Daphne. Pippa could practically see the cogs turning. 'Wait here a moment,' she said suddenly, and went upstairs.

She has got something, thought Pippa. *What will it be? Copies of the letters? Some more poems? Or weekly menus and laundry lists?*

Daphne returned a few minutes later with a small black

book clasped in her hand. 'I'm sorry it isn't more,' she said, 'but I have a volume of Clementina's diary. She asked for it to be destroyed in her will, as she had destroyed all the others, but her executor wanted to preserve it for future generations. Until now, I have respected Clementina's wish that it remain unknown, but if it would help you...'

'I'm sure it will,' said Pippa.

'Please take good care of it,' said Daphne. 'I don't know if you'll find anything much. It's rather domestic, and I don't think it presents Clementina in a very good light, but you can borrow it and show it to Briony if you think that will help. My only request is that you ask me before you make anything public.' She put the journal into Pippa's hand.

Pippa stared at it. 'I – I don't know what to say. Thank you.'

Daphne sighed. 'Maybe I've done the wrong thing in keeping it secret so long. Or maybe I should have burned it, as Clementina wanted. But it's so hard to know what to do.'

'It is,' said Pippa. 'But you've done the right thing.'

'I hope so,' said Daphne. 'Now if you'll excuse me, I might go and have a little lie down. Such a silly thing, but I'm quite done up.'

Pippa put the journal into her bag, said goodbye, and walked home. She felt as if the book were glowing through her bag, and that everyone must know what she had in there. *But I've borrowed it*, she told herself. *I've borrowed it with permission. She sighed. So why do I feel so guilty?*

She visualised Jeremy Lightfoot, tucked away in a

secret studious bookshelf-lined lair, cackling to himself as he analysed Clementina's letters. *You think you've got the better of me*, she thought. *But if I have any say in the matter, you'll be cackling on the other side of your face before I'm finished.*

Chapter 14

'Pippa?' Simon waved his hand in front of Pippa's face, and she jumped.

'What?' she snapped. Then she sighed. 'I'm sorry, I mean good morning.'

'Of course you do.' Simon scrutinised her. 'I was only going to ask if you wanted a cup of tea.' His glance fell on her book. 'It must be a riveting read.'

Pippa put a bookmark carefully between the pages, and closed it. 'I'm not sure I'd say that.'

She had decided not to begin reading the journal the moment she got home from Daphne's. For one thing, there was dinner to make and eat. For another, she didn't want to annoy Simon. And finally, she wanted to enjoy the sense of anticipation before actually opening Clementina Stoate's diary. *Just imagine*, she thought. *An original Victorian diary written by – well, not a famous author, but someone reasonably well known in her day. Jeremy Lightfoot would be so jealous if he knew.* And she had hugged that rather smug feeling close, and let it warm her.

This morning, having woken early and got through the first fifty or so pages of Clementina Stoate's journal, she could acknowledge that another reason for her delay was to put off the possibility that the diary might just be a very dull account of Mrs Stoate's day-to-day life. So far, that was how it was turning out.

She reopened the book. 'Listen to this: *7th February. A damp, miserable day. Charles has yet another cold, and has spent most of the day in bed, complaining and wanting to be made a fuss of. I sat and read to him for an hour, after which he went to sleep. Tried to compose a poem on illness this morning, but no inspiration came despite the obvious exemplar in the house. Embroidered three handkerchiefs with Charles's initials as a present, and gave them to Mary to launder. Roast fowl for dinner, rather dry. I must have a word with Mrs Pargeter.*'

Simon raised his eyebrows. 'The roast fowl isn't the only thing that's dry, then.'

'I know.' Pippa sighed. 'I keep hoping it will improve, but so far it's all like that. I see now what Daphne meant about it being domestic.'

'I'll go and make the tea,' said Simon. 'Please don't read any more out.'

Pippa struggled through a few more pages before it was time to start the day. *Well*, she thought, as she put cereal into bowls and milk into cups, *I've got all morning. Once I've dropped Ruby and Freddie off I can read a bit more. But if it doesn't improve soon, the mystery will be how I manage not to die of boredom.*

Once the children were absorbed into their places of

learning, Pippa headed home. She could feel her pace slowing as she approached the village green. *I could sit in the sun for five minutes*, she thought, then realised that was merely a delaying tactic to avoid getting to grips with Clementina Stoate. *I'd better get it over with*, she thought. *Another fifty pages, and if I haven't found anything significant by then, I'll put it aside and get on with my actual work.*

She went home, made a cup of tea, and settled in her favourite armchair in the sitting room, notepad at the ready.

12th March
Caught Mary reading the newspaper when she was supposed to be laying the drawing-room fire. I am afraid we had an exchange of words. She said that she hadn't expected me to enter the room, given the time of day. I replied that, as the mistress of the household, I may enter any room whenever I wish. I was tempted to box her ears, but refrained.

This is what comes of encouraging servants. Mary came to us with precious little education, and I encouraged her to better herself by joining the circulating library. I even paid for her membership, which, while a trifling expense, is still an expense. However, I felt it was worthwhile, as the servant of a literary figure such as myself should not be ill-informed and illiterate. And this is how she repays me!

In the end I told Mary that if I caught her reading when she ought to be working once more, I would give her notice. That made her saucy look disappear, and I left the room with a sense of a job well done.

Pippa shuddered. Then she picked up a pen and wrote *Encouraged servant Mary to read* in her notepad. After some thought, she added: *Conflict with servant duties.*

She turned the page and continued. The next few pages were commonplace, then Mary's name caught her eye.

27th March

I have taken to my bed absolutely prostrate with nerves. I woke very early, and felt inspiration upon me. Cheered, I left my bed, lit a candle, and went to my writing room. I had in my head a marvellous idea for a poem about a nymph. I had just written down the title, 'Nymph at Play', when I heard a noise downstairs. The clock told me that it was not time for the servants to be rising yet, so early was the hour.

Could it be a burglar? I considered waking Charles; but suspected that as he is often hard to wake, it would be a fruitless endeavour, and the house would be ransacked by the time Charles was ready for action. Therefore I seized the poker, made sure I was well wrapped in my dressing gown, and ventured downstairs.

I heard sounds coming from the kitchen, and revised my guess to that of a tramp or beggar who had broken in looking for food. Heartened by this, I stormed down the corridor, raised the poker, and threw the door open, shouting 'What is the meaning of this?'

If you please, my eye fell on Mary, who had lit a candle

and was feasting upon a thick slice of bread and dripping. I could smell it. 'Sorry, ma'am,' she said, when she had swallowed her mouthful. 'I hope I didn't disturb you.'

'Of course you disturbed me!' I cried. 'I thought you were a burglar.' Then I saw her boots, which were thick with mud. 'Where have you been?' I said. 'And how dare you bring mud into the house like this.'

'I'll clean it up, ma'am,' said Mary, 'soon as I finish breakfast.' She took another mouthful of bread and dripping. 'I went for a walk down to the river. It's nice at this time of day, and it isn't as if I get a walk any other time, is it?'

The cheek of the girl! 'And why did you go for a walk?' I asked. 'Tiring yourself out, when you have a full day of duties ahead of you.'

'It's good for thinking,' she said. 'I sing songs in my head.'

I really didn't know what to say to that. The girl must be possessed. 'That must be cleaned up before Mrs Pargeter comes down,' I said. 'And as for going for walks, I absolutely forbid it, do you hear? Jaunts are for your half day.' And with that, I left.

Of course when I returned to my desk the muse had deserted me, and even the title of my poem seemed weak and lacklustre. I put the sheet of paper in my desk, and closed the drawer on it. Then I went back to bed, but there was no sleep for me; the anger I felt shook me, and I began to cry. Going for a walk to think, forsooth! I suspect that she is meeting a lad.

I shall put extra locks on the doors, and give keys to

Charles and Mrs Pargeter. That should stop any more dawn rambles.

Pippa found her bookmark, and closed the book. She drank some tea, and found her hand was shaking a little. 'What a horrible woman,' she whispered. 'That poor maid.' Then she reflected. *I suppose they were different times. Even so...*

She read on, hoping that Mary would lay low for a bit. Indeed, she seemed to have learnt her lesson, and there was no mention of her for a few pages. Pippa found the dull account of Clementina's life soothing, after the vindictiveness and anger she had shown.

March 31st

Sunday today, and I woke up feeling unwell, so I told Charles that I would not be attending church. He took this with his usual equanimity.

It was rather nice to lie in bed with my breakfast tray and listen to the household going about its business. At length everyone departed for church, and as my headache had abated, I decided to get up. I imagined Charles and the servants all sitting in their pews, and felt pleasantly naughty to have stayed at home. Then I remembered a task I had been meaning to do for a few days. I mounted the back stairs, and entered the servants' bedrooms to conduct an inspection. I am strict about neatness and order, and I shall not have members of my staff behaving like slatterns, even in their own spaces.

As I expected, Mrs Pargeter's room was beyond

reproach. Her bed was made, her clothes neatly put away, and her Bible lay on her bedside table.

Then I came to the room which Mary and Abigail share, and I am sorry to report that it was a very different story. Abigail's side of the room was quite neat, barring some woollen stockings which had been carelessly thrust into a drawer rather than being neatly rolled, but Mary's side of the room was a pigsty. Her uniform was hung up carelessly, and her work boots lay where she had obviously discarded them the night before, and were sorely in need of a clean and polish. Her bedside table, moreover, was littered with cheap magazines and pieces of paper covered in scribbles. Letters, so carelessly scrawled that they were not fit to send. I picked up the whole heap, took it to my room, and cast it into the fire. That girl is a disgrace.

By the time Charles returned from church, my headache was completely gone. Indeed, I felt well enough to dress, and even to begin the composition of a poem.

The effect of a little time to oneself is truly wonderful. I must make sure I indulge myself more often.

'I really hope you don't,' muttered Pippa, with a prickling sense of unease. She glanced at the clock. The time she had planned to spend on the journal was almost gone. *I'll just read a few more pages.*

There wasn't much left of the book now, and the entries had grown comparatively sparse. Pippa scanned the pages, both looking for Mary's name and hoping not to find it. Then she came to an entry headed *A terrible day*, and gasped.

July 24

Mary, our maid, is dead. She was missed at breakfast. Mrs Pargeter thought she might have gone for a walk, but I told her sharply that I had forbidden such activities. I thought the silly girl had run away, quite possibly with a young man. I remain convinced that she has been conducting a secret relationship. I had not recorded it here because one's diary ought to be a place of comfort and rest, not of vulgar speculation.

Charles insisted she should be looked for. Little Abigail volunteered that Mary liked to walk by the river. She said she would go and see if Mary had perhaps fallen asleep on the bank. Not more than a quarter of an hour later, she ran in sobbing. 'She's in the river, she's in the river!'

Charles sent his valet William to get the policeman, and when he came Charles went down with them himself. He is such a kind and considerate master. When he returned, he told me that Mary had drowned. They pulled the body out, and found no marks of violence upon her. I suspect the unhappy wretch drowned herself, possibly because she was with child. At any rate, it is a terrible shame and a warning to young women everywhere.

Pippa slammed the book shut, fumbled for a tissue, and burst into tears. Once she had recovered, she reached for her mobile phone. She found the number she wanted, and dialled.

'Good morning—'

'I need to speak to Briony Shepherd, please. It's urgent.'

Chapter 15

'When you said you knew just the place,' said Briony, 'this isn't exactly what I had in mind.' She grimaced at her cup. 'I asked for a flat white, what's this supposed to be?'

'Sorry,' said Pippa. 'But the point is, none of your students or your colleagues will be here.'

'I very much doubt it,' said Briony. 'All right, we've got three quarters of an hour and I've put my phone on silent. What is it?'

Pippa looked around. The Coffee Pot was deserted apart from themselves and a mournful-looking server. She delved in her bag and brought out the journal. 'Daphne gave me this,' she said, and laid Clementina Stoate's journal on the table.

Briony frowned at it. 'What…?' She opened it, glanced at the first page, and stared at Pippa. 'You're kidding me. I didn't even know this existed.'

'No one does,' said Pippa. 'Daphne let me borrow it, and she said you could read it too, as long as we don't share it any wider without permission. Most of it's dull as dishwater, but towards the end...' She looked around again before leaning forward. 'Clementina Stoate had a maid, Mary. They didn't get on. The maid kept pushing her luck, and Clementina kept putting her in her place. I think she enjoyed it. It was around then that Clementina's poetry started to take off. Suddenly, Mary was found dead in the river. Clementina wrote that she thought Mary had drowned herself because she was pregnant, but I don't know. And it's all... It's all very odd.'

'Mmm,' said Briony. 'Can you show me those bits?'

Pippa took back the book and riffled through the pages, seeking the entries she had read only a short time ago. 'Here,' she said, pointing. 'In this one Clementina sneaked into the servants' bedrooms when everyone was at church, and burnt Mary's magazines and letters because her room was untidy. And then she went off and wrote a poem.'

'I'll never be rude about my head of department again,' said Briony. She read through the entry, then took out her phone. 'Mind if I take a picture?'

'No, go ahead,' said Pippa. 'Just be careful of the book.'

'I shall.' Briony held the page down carefully, and took a snap. 'Show me the entry about Mary's death.'

Pippa found it. Briony read it quickly, then took another photo. 'So do you think Clementina Stoate got some sort of weird poetic inspiration by being horrible to her maid?'

Pippa shrugged. 'I don't know if that's the reason, but it seemed to happen at around the same time.'

'And in the absence of any other explanation, I guess it's worth investigating.' Briony's eyes had a strange, possessive gleam. 'God, I'd love to shut myself away with this for a few days and see what I could tease out.'

'I know,' said Pippa. 'I wish I could let you have it, but I can't. I promised Daphne that I'd take care of it, and after the letters...'

Briony sighed. 'That git Lightfoot.' She sipped her coffee and made a face. 'But if he hadn't taken the letters, we'd never have got hold of this journal. And we know the letters are missing, but he doesn't even know this journal exists.' She gave Pippa a conspiratorial look. 'So I guess we're ahead.'

'Never mind who's ahead,' said Pippa, 'what do we do now?'

'Think,' said Briony. She looked at her watch. 'We haven't got long. When did all this kick off between Clementina and her maid?'

Pippa thought. 'I don't think Clementina ever had a high opinion of her. But I think it started when she caught Mary reading the newspaper. Here, I'll show you.' She found the page, and Briony took another photo.

'Right, so that was the twelfth of March, and Mary was dead a few months later,' said Briony.

Pippa shivered. 'Yes.'

'But the thing is,' said Briony, 'that Clementina continued to write good poems after Mary had died. So I'm not sure that your hypothesis holds up.'

'Are you like this in class?' said Pippa.

'Sometimes,' said Briony. 'I just can't let you make an assertion without the evidence to back it up.'

'So what must I do to satisfy you, Dr Shepherd?' said

Pippa.

'Don't be snarky,' said Briony. 'OK, what I'll do now is get snaps of every page from when Clementina and Mary fell out, up to her death. That way I've got something to work on too. And also, if anything does happen to the journal, at least we've got a backup of sorts.'

'That's a good idea,' said Pippa. She drank her tea and watched Briony work through the journal. 'She had very nice handwriting, didn't she?'

'People often did then, if they could write,' said Briony. 'I mean, it isn't as if they could type things out. They had to write legibly, and they were taught to write appropriately for their station. I imagine Clementina learned ladies'-hand from her governess.' She took another picture. 'If you look at Victorian manuscripts, they are often neatly written, with no more than a few corrections. It's almost unimaginable now, when we're so used to being able to delete and retype.'

'Isn't it,' said Pippa. Briony turned the page, and she studied it upside-down. 'There are no crossings-out at all.'

'Like I said, different times,' said Briony, her focus entirely on the book.

'So what do I do,' said Pippa, 'apart from wait for your opinion?'

'What I'd like you to do,' said Briony, 'is have a really good look at the entries after Mary's death. That will tell us about Clementina's creative process. Hopefully, there'll be clues to what drove her. From what I remember, she stopped writing when her husband died, so the critical view, such as it is, is that his death killed her inspiration.'

'OK,' said Pippa. 'That doesn't sound too difficult. The entries get shorter anyway.'

'Then we have a plan,' said Briony. 'Or at least, the beginnings of one.' She held out a hand. 'Shake on it.'

Pippa did as she was told, feeling silly. 'You make it seem like a secret pact.'

'Maybe it is,' said Briony. 'An academic investigative sisterhood.'

'Gosh,' said Pippa. She wanted to laugh, but Briony looked very earnest.

'When shall we check in?' said Briony. 'And how do we do it? I'm not sure we should commit anything to email.'

'We could phone each other,' said Pippa. 'Unless you think Jeremy Lightfoot might tap our phones.'

'I bet he would if he knew how,' said Briony. 'OK, if you come up with anything, text me and ask for a meeting. Don't say why. This is my mobile number.' She called it up on her phone and Pippa typed it in.

'Got it. I'll send you a text, and then you've got mine.' Pippa typed *Hello*, pressed *Send*, and Briony's phone buzzed.

'Contact made,' said Briony. She continued photographing the pages of the journal.

'I wish we could interview people,' said Pippa. 'Find out what Mary was like, find out what the other servants thought of her, and whether she was as wayward as Clementina says.'

'Clementina probably thought she was,' said Briony. 'It was a different world then. How old was Mary?'

'I'm not sure... I'll see if I can find out,' said Pippa. 'I remember from that letter Jeremy Lightfoot read out that she was an ex-workhouse girl. That sounds as if she was young.'

'She could have been in her late teens, even,' said Briony. 'Some of her behaviour we'd probably class as normal teenage acting-out nowadays, but it would have been a class and gender thing too. Servants would have had very little freedom in many households. And the mistress of the house might suspect a female servant of carrying on with the master, particularly if they were young and attractive.' She looked thoughtful. 'Maybe that was an angle.'

Pippa sighed. 'There's a lot to think about, isn't there?'

Briony laughed. 'Imagine if we had the letters to go through as well.'

'Oh, don't,' said Pippa. 'I wonder...'

Briony took another photo. 'I think that's all of them,' she said. She closed the book and pushed it towards Pippa. 'You wonder what?'

'I wonder, if Jeremy Lightfoot knew what we know about Clementina Stoate, whether he'd still want to do his literary festival.'

Briony snorted. 'He'd probably airbrush that out. I don't think his research interests include power struggles and sadism.'

'I wonder whether the letters contain the same sort of information,' said Pippa. Then she gasped. 'What if – what if he censors them?'

'What do you mean?' asked Briony, frowning. 'You

mean he might suppress things?'

'Worse than that,' said Pippa. 'I mean destroy things. I bet Daphne has no idea how many letters are in that folder. All he'd need to do is take out any letters that didn't fit his theory and shred them.'

'Woah,' said Briony. 'We've got to get them back.'

'We don't know he's got them,' said Pippa uncertainly. 'I mean, we don't have proof, however much we think that's the case.'

'It's so frustrating.' Briony looked at her phone. 'And speaking of frustrating, I'd better get back to campus.'

'And I'd better go and pick up Ruby,' said Pippa. 'I don't know when I'll be able to work on the journal, but I'll try as hard as I can.'

'I know you will,' said Briony. 'We're in this together. Odd Couple Investigators, Inc.'

Pippa walked to her car, her mind whirling. Were they on the right lines? Was she barking up the wrong tree completely? *I'd like to get Clementina Stoate in an interview room and give her a damn good interrogation*, she thought grimly.

She'd cut it fine, and had to drive straight to nursery, where Rach greeted her with smiles. 'She's been ever so good today,' she said. 'And she wrote E, F, *and* G.'

'Wonderful,' said Pippa, remembering Clementina Stoate's neat, flawless script.

She made a big fuss of Ruby to compensate for the fact that she would much rather be working on Clementina's journal than entertaining her daughter solo for the next three hours or so.

'Can we have special lunch? Because I was good?' asked Ruby, bouncing along beside her.

'We'll have to see,' said Pippa. 'I'll have a look when we get home and see what I can rustle up.' That satisfied Ruby, and she submitted to being buckled into her car seat quite happily.

As an extra treat, when they got home Pippa put on Ruby's DVD. 'Just while I'm making lunch, mind,' she said. 'And afterwards, I want you to write EFG for me.'

'I will, Mummy,' said Ruby, looking angelic.

Pippa smiled at her, and went into the kitchen. There was nothing particularly exciting in the fridge, but she found a packet of fish fingers in the freezer. 'Fish finger sandwich with tomato sauce?' she called.

'Yes please, Mummy!'

So easily pleased, thought Pippa. She set the grill to heat and counted out fish fingers, with Clementina's journal entries running through her mind like some sort of Victorian news ticker. It kept going as she put the fish fingers in to cook, turned them, got plates, buttered bread... It was only when she went to the cupboard for the tomato sauce that she saw the handle of the back door hanging down like a broken limb.

Chapter 16

'Good afternoon, Much Gadding pol—'

'It's Pippa Parker. Someone's tried to break into my house. Can you come round and check for fingerprints?'

'Yes Mrs Parker, I'll come round immediately.' PC Gannet sounded rather pleased. 'Can I have your address?'

Pippa reeled it off. 'Could you knock quietly, please? My daughter is here and I don't want to worry her.'

'Yes ma'am,' said PC Gannet. 'I'll be there as soon as I can.'

Pippa spent the intervening few minutes going into each room and checking off their belongings. Everything was in its usual sort of order; in other words, not much order at all. The TV and DVD player were there, obviously; her laptop was still in its bag in the dining room; her jewellery box undisturbed. She heard a quiet tap at the door and ran downstairs. A lanky form wearing a hat was visible through the etched glass. It couldn't be anyone else.

Pippa stepped out and pushed the door to behind her. 'Where did they get in?' said PC Gannet. 'I take it it wasn't this door.' He gave her a stern glance. 'You didn't leave a window open, did you?'

'It's the back door,' said Pippa. 'And now I've checked round the house, I don't think they got in. I tried the door on the kitchen side and it's still locked, but the handle is knackered.'

'I see,' said PC Gannet, looking disappointed. 'Can I get round the back?'

'Yes, there's a gate,' said Pippa. 'I'll go through and let you in. Assuming I can get the door open.'

'Mummy, what's that smell?' called Ruby.

Pippa sniffed. 'Damn! I mean, whoops. You don't mind your fish fingers well done, do you Ruby?'

'Oh, Mummy,' sighed Ruby.

Pippa ran into the kitchen and extinguished the grill. To be fair, the fish fingers were browner than usual, but salvageable. She rummaged through the kitchen drawer for the back-door key, which as usual was right at the bottom, put it in the lock, and prayed. It turned, and the door swung open without any further effort from Pippa.

She heard a cough from behind the gate, and let PC Gannet in. Pippa noticed he was carrying a small bag, and suspected he had had it packed and ready ever since he had taken command at Much Gadding. *A bit like my hospital bag when I was pregnant with Freddie.*

'Is this the door?' said PC Gannet, nodding at it.

'That's the one,' said Pippa. 'They've broken the handle, but the lock seems to work.'

PC Gannet eyed it critically, then opened his bag and took out a pair of gloves. 'You'll need to get that replaced.'

'Um, would you like a cup of tea?' Pippa asked.

PC Gannet stared at her as if this was the most ridiculous thing he'd ever heard. 'No, thank you.'

Feeling thoroughly dismissed, Pippa went inside. She pulled the door closed, and it swung open again. 'I'll have to lock this to keep it closed,' she said. 'Is that all right?'

PC Gannet raised his eyebrows, which she assumed was a yes.

Pippa ate a piece of fish finger for quality control purposes. *Not my finest cuisine, but it'll do.* She made the sandwiches, including hefty dollops of ketchup to disguise the burnt bits, and took them into the sitting room. 'Lunch time.'

Ruby goggled at the plates. 'We don't eat in here.'

'Well, today we do. It's part of your treat for being good,' said Pippa.

'Oh. OK,' said Ruby, and turned back to the screen.

Pippa finished her sandwich and got up to take the plate to the kitchen. She almost dropped it as a shape loomed through the kitchen window at her. 'Aaaah!' she cried.

'What is it, Mummy?' Ruby called. 'Did you fall?'

'No, Ruby,' said Pippa, pressing a hand to her thumping heart. 'I just – thought I saw something. But I didn't. Nothing.'

There was no response.

Pippa unlocked the door and glared at PC Gannet. 'You nearly gave me a heart attack,' she muttered.

'Sorry about that,' said PC Gannet, looking less than contrite. 'I'm afraid there aren't any prints on the door handle or the lock. I imagine whoever did it wore gloves, and they probably wiped it too. Clearly professionals.' He nodded respectfully.

'But if they were professionals,' said Pippa, 'how come they couldn't get in? I mean, it's not a particularly sophisticated lock. We never thought it would need to be.'

'I bet you've changed your mind about that now,' said PC Gannet. He peeled off his gloves, put them in the bag, and took out his notebook. 'If you don't mind, I'll take a few details. When did you leave the house?'

Pippa considered. 'I think a little before ten.'

PC Gannet made a note. 'And there was nothing wrong with the door handle at that time?'

'I certainly didn't notice anything,' said Pippa. 'I made a cup of tea, and everything seemed all right then.'

'And when did you return home?'

'Just after half twelve. I saw the door when I came into the kitchen to make lunch, and I rang you straight away.'

'Good,' said PC Gannet. 'That was the right thing to do.' He fixed her with a penetrating stare. 'And you're reasonably sure that no one has managed to get into the house?'

'Yes,' said Pippa. 'The door was still locked, and nothing's been taken.'

PC Gannet snapped his notebook shut. 'You've had a very lucky escape,' he said. 'I'd advise you to get that door mechanism replaced ASAP.' He rocked on the balls of his feet. 'I shall speak to your neighbours and ascertain whether they saw anything between the times you have mentioned, and I will also put a warning notice on the Much Gadding police social media feeds.'

'Thank you,' said Pippa.

'I'll see myself out,' said PC Gannet. He tipped his hat to Pippa, and walked briskly through the garden gate.

Pippa had a terrible urge to giggle, and also to cry, but managed to suppress both. *Not in front of Ruby*. She bolted the gate behind PC Gannet, and went back into the house. On the hall table was the latest copy of the local magazine, *Much Gadding Life*. She scanned the small ads and went to get her phone from the sitting room.

'Working, Mummy?' said Ruby, scrutinising her.

'No,' said Pippa. 'I just need to make a quick call.'

Stan Stan the Locksmith Man, as he advertised himself, breathed rather heavily as Pippa explained her problem. 'I see,' he said. 'That isn't good, is it?'

'No, it isn't,' said Pippa. 'Can you come out and fix it?'

'I'm on a job at the moment, love,' said Stan, 'but I could get to you for three.'

'Oh,' said Pippa. 'That's a bit close to school pick-up time.'

'That's all I've got till after the weekend,' said Stan. 'Unless you want to pay an out of hours surcharge.'

'Three o'clock would be lovely,' said Pippa.

Her next job was to ring Sheila and beg a favour. 'I wouldn't ask,' she said, 'but something's wrong with the back door, and obviously I can't go out with it like that.'

'Ooh no, you can't,' said Sheila. 'You can never be too careful.' She paused. 'You don't think someone's been trying to get in, do you?'

Pippa crossed her fingers behind her back. 'Nooooo, I don't think we've got anything a burglar would want to steal. It's probably one of the kids hanging off it.'

'Mmm,' said Sheila. 'I hope so.' She sighed. 'Shall I bring Freddie straight to yours, or keep him for his tea?'

'Oh no, don't go to any trouble,' said Pippa. 'Straight back here is fine.'

Sheila made a noise which sounded as if it meant *I should think not.* 'I'll see you at about half past three, then.'

'Thanks Sheila, I'll get the kettle on for you.'

Pippa ended the call and slumped in her chair. *Hopefully the house will be secure by the time Simon gets home.* That was a point, she should probably text him. She pinched the bridge of her nose, and picked up her phone again.

Someone tried to break in while I was out this morning, but they didn't manage it. Getting lock replaced this afternoon. Nothing missing. Love you P x

***

She heard Simon's car pull up outside and looked at her watch. 'Four thirty?' she said. 'He's never home at four thirty.'

Not even on a Friday. Pippa waited for him to open the door, but it didn't happen. In the end she opened the front door and peered out. Simon had been apprehended by Sandy, their next-door neighbour, who was holding forth with a great deal of hand-waving.

'It's terrible isn't it, absolutely terrible. We aren't safe in our own homes. Anyway, that's decided me. I'm getting a security camera. It's the only way. But as I told PC Gannet, I didn't see a thing. I'm just thankful they didn't try and get into my house. I think that fake alarm box I've got put them off. You should get one.'

'Perhaps we should,' said Simon, looking as if he had stepped into a wind tunnel by mistake. 'I'll bear it in mind.' He glanced up and saw Pippa. 'I'll go and see how my wife is. She might need calming down.' Pippa obligingly assumed a worried expression.

'You weren't in the house, were you?' said Sandy. 'That's my worst nightmare, hearing someone breaking in, and running to hide, and lying under the bed listening to them rummage through my belongings—'

'No, I wasn't in,' said Pippa. 'And they didn't get in. They just tried to. And we've got a new lock on the back door. But yes, Simon, I need to tell you about it. Inside.'

Simon shot a *You see?* expression at Sandy, and hurried into the house. 'Good grief,' he said. 'That woman can talk for England. Shame she was out shopping when it happened. She's probably kicking herself.' He looked at Pippa. 'Anyway, are you all right? I tried to ring, but it went to voicemail.'

'Oh, sorry,' said Pippa, 'I had the phone on silent. Ruby was being a bit needy. But she can write a very good E, F and G. She's written lots of them. For most of the afternoon.'

'It's been a good day, then,' said Simon. 'Come on, show me this famous lock.'

Pippa led the way to the kitchen and pointed at the back door, which now boasted a new handle, two locks, bolts top and bottom, and a chain.

'Wow,' said Simon. 'He didn't do things by halves.'

'I got talked into the door chain,' said Pippa. 'I have no idea when we'll ever use it, but hey. Stan didn't charge the earth, so I let him have his way.'

'And you're sure that nothing is missing?' said Simon.

'As sure as I can be,' said Pippa. 'The door was still locked when I got in. It was just the handle that was broken.'

'I wonder what they were after,' said Simon. 'I'd have thought if they were trying to break in anywhere, they would go for the big new houses on the posh estate.'

'I suppose,' said Pippa. 'Anyway, do you fancy takeaway pizza tonight? It's been a strange day, and I can't say I feel like cooking.'

Simon grinned. 'Do you ever feel like cooking?' Then the grin disappeared. 'I'm glad you're all right, though. I was worried.' He folded her in a hug. 'It is odd, though. Sandy next door said she'd spoken to the neighbour on her other side, and Karen on our right, and they haven't been targeted. And Karen's back door looks as if you could blow it down with one breath.'

'Just one of those things, I guess,' said Pippa. 'I'll go and find the pizza menu.'

'Good idea,' said Simon. 'I'll go and get changed. At least the weekend came early.'

Pippa found the menu and took it into the dining room. She could feel her face heating up. It could be a random burglar; or it could be someone looking for a thing no normal burglar would want. She went into the hallway, took the journal from her bag, and stared at it. *Is this what they were after?*

Chapter 17

The alarm couldn't sound quickly enough for Pippa on Monday morning. As soon as the radio came on she was out of bed and heading downstairs towards caffeine.

'You're lively,' called Simon. 'What's brought this on?'

'Oh, you know,' said Pippa. 'New week, full of opportunities.' She heard a low *Ugh* as she switched on the kettle.

It had been a frustrating, jumpy sort of weekend. On one hand she was desperate to delve into Clementina's journal; but that wasn't compatible with two small children, all the weekend jobs, or the big shop.

And on the other hand, there was Simon. Pippa tried to convince herself that the journal and the attempted break-in were in no way related, but she couldn't help wondering... And she had a distinct feeling that if she spent too much time poring over the journal, Simon would put two and two together and make a very convincing four out of them. Pippa wasn't sure what would happen then; but she had no intention of returning the journal to Daphne before she had worked out what was going on. So she had slipped the journal into her laptop bag, and tried to ignore it. Every so often she would go into the dining room, where the bag lived, and check that it was still there.

But now the weekend was over, and she had the prospect of a whole morning to herself once the children had been dropped off. *What shall I find? Perhaps today is the day we solve the mystery.* She hugged herself, imagining Briony delivering a fascinating lecture on the subject at the literary festival which she would organise, and which, if she had her way, Jeremy Lightfoot would have no part in. *I must see about him*, she thought. *Perhaps another email.*

The children sensed Pippa's impatience, too. 'Are you doing something today, Mummy?', asked Freddie as she did up his polo shirt, because she couldn't stand watching him fumble with the buttons a moment longer.

'Not particularly,' said Pippa. 'Just keen to get started. I think it'll be an interesting day.'

'We're having an interesting day,' said Freddie. 'We're playing killerball with Mrs Simmons.'

'I hope that's less worrying than it sounds,' said Pippa.

Freddie giggled. 'No one gets killed, Mummy,' he said. 'Don't be silly.'

Freddie was, at length, delivered to his classroom, and Pippa steered Ruby around the little groups of mums chatting in the playground. 'Come along, Ruby,' she said. 'Things to do.'

Alicia opened the nursery door. 'Hello, Ruby,' she said. 'You're with me today.'

Ruby stared up at her. 'Not Cygnets?'

'No, you don't have to go to Cygnets today,' said Alicia. 'You can stay with me.'

'But I like Cygnets,' said Ruby.

'Well,' said Alicia, taking her hand and opening the Duckling Room door, 'why don't you do some colouring with Becky, and we'll see how we get on.' Ruby still looked uncertain, but after a cuddle and kiss from Pippa she went willingly enough.

'I'm confused,' said Pippa. 'I thought Mrs Snell wanted Ruby to go into Cygnets.'

'Oh, she did,' said Alicia. 'But the Taylors have left. Joshua and Jemima. You know.'

Pippa had a vague impression of blonde twins in the Duckling Room. 'I think so.'

'Yes, Mr Taylor's been posted overseas, and they've all gone with him. It was on, then off, then suddenly it was on again. So now there's plenty of room with me, and you don't have to worry.'

'Oh,' said Pippa. 'Um, thanks.'

'I'll let you get on,' said Alicia, and Pippa had no choice but to go.

Pippa turned over the question of Ducklings versus Cygnets most of the way home, coming to no conclusions. *Let's see how it goes today*, she thought. *Then I've got something to go on.* The matter shelved, she let herself in, checked the back door, and settled in the dining room with the journal.

What had Briony said? *Look at the entries after Mary's death.* Pippa shrugged, and leafed through the journal until she came to the right place. The next entry was a week later.

Mary has been buried. Reverend Halsey was reluctant to put her in the churchyard, as he said there was too much doubt about the manner of her death. He said that if Charles insisted, Mary would have to be buried by the churchyard wall, at night, with no Christian rites. Charles tried to reason with him, but he stood firm. So Charles found a spot under an oak tree, six feet outside the churchyard wall, and paid some money to the gravedigger.

He asked the Reverend to at least read a prayer over the grave, but he absolutely refused. So Charles did it. He told me that it was a sad affair; no family of course, a plain coffin, and then just himself, and the servants who felt they could bear it. Little Abigail did not go. Of course I did not attend; my nerves would have been shattered.

I had thought of seeing if Abigail could move up to housemaid, but she is too young. I shall advertise in the newspaper and ask around. I do not think I could bear another workhouse girl.

Pippa pushed the book away. 'How could she?' she muttered. 'That poor girl is barely in the ground.'

The next entry was two weeks later.

Mr Chapman has written to ask if I would care to send him a poem for the next issue of his magazine. Apparently the ones I sent were a great success, and he has had many complimentary letters about them. I am not sure I am equal to composition, given all the recent trouble and disturbance, but I must do my best. I shall go for a walk tomorrow morning and contemplate nature.

Pippa turned the page expecting to hear more, but the next entry was ten days afterwards.

Mr Chapman has accepted my poem, and offered me five pounds for it! I am in ecstasy! Of course the money is not really important; but I have never received such a sum for a published work before. That will pay half of Abigail's wage for the year. Never again will Charles be able to frown at me when I withdraw to my room to write, or seem absent-minded, for I am contributing to the household.

Mr Chapman also sent me a package of letters from admirers. I confess that as I read I hugged each one to my bosom, and almost cried. What joy to be able to bring happiness to people through the written word!

He has also asked, very respectfully, whether I would consider travelling to London to attend a literary salon. He even held out the prospect of meeting Mr Browning. I think I must decline, for I do not feel equal to such an ordeal, but it is nice to be asked. I shall sleep on it.

'Fame at last,' murmured Pippa. She read on, and found much of the same: requests for more poems, praise from fans, a short account of Clementina's attendance at the salon (Mr Browning was otherwise engaged), and a poetry reading at the parish hall, which was apparently received with great delight by all who attended. But nothing was said about the composition of the poems, apart from occasional references to 'natural inspiration' and 'creative fire'.

After another few pages of this, Pippa began to feel nauseous. *I need to clear my head*, she thought. Then an idea occurred to her. Why not take a walk herself and seek inspiration from Clementina's house, and the roads she walked on? *At least it will get me out of the house.* Pippa put her trainers on, checked the back door once again for good measure, and set off at a brisk pace.

She slowed down as she came to Clementina's house, as she now thought of it. It looked just the same as ever on the outside: the small-paned windows, the timbering, the uncompromising front door... Pippa tried to imagine Clementina sitting at the desk she had seen and working on her poetry; perhaps dipping her pen, or pausing for thought. Yet somehow she found it hard to visualise. She shrugged, and moved on. *I know she went to the green*, she thought. *She definitely mentioned that.*

Pippa wandered across the road and onto the well-kept grass. A few daisies had had the audacity to pop up here and there, and the effect was rather cheering.

'Good heavens,' said a friendly voice from a nearby bench.

Pippa looked down, and recognised Gerry the milkman from choir. 'Oh, hello Gerry,' she said. 'Sorry, I didn't see you there.'

'I almost thought you were a ghost,' said Gerry. 'It's been that long since you've come to choir.'

Pippa grimaced. 'Don't remind me. I'm surprised Jen

hasn't sent out a search party to press-gang me back in.'

'Now there's a good idea,' said Gerry, with a grin. 'Funny, isn't it. You're reminded of someone, and then they start popping up everywhere.'

'Who, Jen?'

'No, you,' said Gerry. 'I was talking about you on Friday. I remember thinking that your ears must be burning.'

'Only good things, I hope,' said Pippa. 'Who were you talking to?'

'Oh, just some chap,' said Gerry. 'I'd finished my round and I was heading back when I spotted him looking lost. He asked if I could tell him the way to St Stephen's Church, and I said if he was after that he'd have a long walk, because we haven't got one of those. I told him where St Saviour's was.'

'I don't understand,' said Pippa. 'Where did I come into it?'

'Oh, he said that you'd told him it had wonderful stained glass. Well, he said a lady named Pippa. At least, he thought it was Pippa, and you're the only Pippa I know in the village. So I said, "Was that Pippa Parker?", and he said that sounded right. Anyway, he said he'd try to look you up, so I told him your road, and said there'd be a red Mini parked outside if you were in.' Gerry eyed Pippa. 'I take it he didn't find you?'

'I didn't see him, certainly,' said Pippa. 'What did he look like, this chap?'

'Familiar,' said Gerry. 'I can't put my finger on it, but I'm sure I've seen him somewhere. Tall chap, middle-aged and a bit dashing. He was wearing red trousers, which I thought was rather bold.'

'And he wasn't local,' said Pippa.

'Bit hard to tell,' said Gerry. 'He didn't have a Gadcestershire accent, but not everyone does. He had a cultured voice, I'd say.' He laughed. 'Anyway, when he does track you down he'll probably tell you off for sending him to the wrong church! He looked like the sort of chap who'd be particular about that sort of thing.'

'Did he,' said Pippa grimly. 'It's been nice to catch up, Gerry, but I'd better get back to work.' She got up from the bench and strolled off in as nonchalant a manner as she possibly could until she judged she was out of Gerry's sight. Then she broke into a run.

Jim picked up the third time she rang. 'Can I call you back?' he said.

'Yes,' said Pippa, 'but I've got a job for you. Someone tried to break into my house last Friday, and now I know who it was. And if he did that, then I'm convinced he's got those letters too.'

'I'll call you straight back when I'm done here,' said Jim. 'Got a name for me?'

'I certainly have,' said Pippa. 'Jeremy Lightfoot.'

Chapter 18

'I'm sorry, Pippa, but I'm really not convinced,' said Jim.

'Why don't you see?' Pippa snapped down the phone. 'It's got to be him! Who else could it be?'

'I think you're assuming too many things,' said Jim. 'All right, let's go back to Gerry. What description did he give you of the man he spoke to?'

'Middle-aged, dashing, posh voice, wearing red trousers,' said Pippa. 'That sounds exactly like Jeremy Lightfoot. And you must admit it's a bit suspicious, wandering around a strange village at what, seven thirty in the morning.'

'It's hardly a watertight identification, is it?' said Jim.

'But this guy practically asked for me by name!' cried Pippa.

Jim sighed. 'OK. Can you go through the conversation for me again, exactly as you remember it.'

When Pippa had finished, he said nothing for a few moments.

'I take it you're still not convinced,' said Pippa.

'It's all a bit up in the air,' Jim replied. 'The guy mentioned someone who might have been called Pippa, and naturally, because Gerry knows you, he assumed that was you and gave the man your surname, and the man agreed that sounded right. It isn't as if the chap went up to Gerry and asked him if he knew someone called Pippa Parker who lived in the village, now is it?'

'I still think it's him,' grumbled Pippa.

'Look,' said Jim, 'I can get out of the office for a couple of hours. If you get hold of Gerry, I'll interview him at the police station. And if there's something to go on, we can take it from there.'

'Really?' asked Pippa.

'Yes, really,' said Jim. 'If it was anybody else I'd probably tell them to come back with proper evidence, but given your disturbing tendency to be right most of the time, I'm prepared to take it seriously. Go and track down your man, and let me know where I can find you both.'

'Thanks, Jim,' said Pippa, but Jim had already rung off.

Pippa dashed out of the house, hoping that Gerry would still be at the green. The bench where he had been sitting was empty; but she saw a figure crossing the road towards the library. 'Wait!' she shouted, and set off in pursuit.

She caught up with Gerry at the door of the library. 'Are you all right?' he asked, frowning. 'You look as if the hounds of hell were after you.'

'Not quite that,' said Pippa. 'I need you to talk to PC Horsley. He's on his way.'

'Jim Horsley?' said Gerry. 'Why, what have I done now?'

'Not you,' said Pippa. 'The chap you were talking to on Friday. I think he tried to break into my house.'

'Oh,' said Gerry. 'Oh dear.' He stood at the door of the library, looking worried. 'Do I go to the police station?'

'Not yet,' said Pippa. 'Jim's got to drive from Gadcester, so you could go and get your book.'

Gerry shook his head. 'I don't think I'm in the mood.'

'We can sit on the green, then,' said Pippa. 'I'll text Jim and tell him where we are.'

She received no reply to her text. *He must be driving*, she thought, and a wave of uncertainty rippled through her. What if she had got it wrong? What if Gerry had misremembered? *But it's got to be him*, a little voice in her head said. *Who else would have the nerve to do such a thing?*

She and Gerry sat at opposite ends of the same bench. Occasionally one of them volunteered an item of small talk, but mostly they were quiet. There didn't seem to be much to say.

Eventually Pippa's phone buzzed. *At MG station and have explained to Gannet. Please bring witness with you.*

On our way, replied Pippa. She put her phone away and got up. 'It's time, Gerry.'

When they arrived at the police station PC Gannet was nowhere to be seen. 'I sent him for a break,' said Jim. 'Come through, please. No, not you, Mrs Parker. Just . . . is it Gerry?'

Gerry looked extremely uncomfortable. 'That's right, Jim. I hope I haven't done anything I shouldn't.'

'I wouldn't have thought so,' said Jim. 'I doubt we'll be

long. Mrs Parker, please wait here.'

Pippa watched the hands of the clock crawl round. For variety she read the posters on the wall, then flicked through a large-format newsletter about policing in Gadcestershire. Even reading slowly, that took no more than five minutes. She strained her ears to hear what was going on in the back room, but heard nothing. Then she thought of all the work she could be doing, and wondered how Ruby was getting on in Ducklings. Then, unable to settle, she took out her phone and played solitaire.

She was on her third game when the door opened. 'All done,' said Jim. 'Thanks for your assistance, Gerry. I don't think we'll need to be in touch, but if we do, I've got your number.'

'Thank you very much,' said Gerry, as if he wanted to touch a hat he wasn't wearing. He nodded to Pippa, then walked briskly to the door, and left.

'Well?' said Pippa.

Jim shrugged. 'It isn't conclusive. I showed Gerry a photo of Jeremy Lightfoot, and even found a clip of him talking on YouTube, but Gerry couldn't be sure that was the man. He said it was like him, but he couldn't swear to it. Apparently the man he spoke to was wearing a hat and his face was in shadow, which of course complicates matters.'

'You should pull him in for questioning,' said Pippa. 'When I think of his behaviour that evening at Daphne's house, he was definitely up to something. I should have realised when he pretended to have lost his laptop. And thinking about it, he was the only person who had a bag the right size to take that file of letters.'

'Mmm,' said Jim. 'I think we ought to leave the file aside for now. So what was his motive for breaking into your house?'

'Daphne lent me a journal written by Clementina Stoate,' said Pippa. 'It's a secret, but he must have found out somehow that I've got it, and decided to steal it. That's why he was asking for directions to my house, because of course he doesn't know where I live.'

'But how would he know that you have this journal?' said Jim.

'I don't know,' said Pippa. 'Perhaps Daphne let something slip when he was speaking to her. Or maybe there's a reference to it in one of the letters that he stole.' She looked up to find Jim studying her. 'What?'

'You're clutching at straws, Pippa,' he said. 'You want it to be this Jeremy Lightfoot guy, and you're bending the evidence to fit your theory. That's the wrong way round.'

'What am I supposed to think?' cried Pippa. 'I've tried to get hold of him, and he is apparently on *study leave*. It doesn't take a genius to work out what he's doing.' She glared at him. 'You know what? If you won't help, I'll get hold of him myself.' Pippa grabbed her phone and scrolled through her list of contacts. 'Hello, Beryl? Sorry to bother you, but could I speak to Lady Higginbotham? It's rather urgent. Yes, I'll hold.' She drummed her fingers on the next chair as she waited. 'Hello, Lady Higginbotham? It's Pippa. I believe you have Jeremy Lightfoot's phone number, and I need to speak to him. Yes, I've got pencil and paper.' She gestured at Jim to pass her some, then scribbled a number down. 'Yes, I've got it. Thanks ever so much. Yes, I'll be in touch soon about the Proms. No, I haven't forgotten. Must go, bye.' She glanced at Jim smugly. 'Now we'll see.'

'Are you sure this is a good idea?' said Jim.

Pippa shrugged. 'Well, if you won't help me—' She dialled the number, and put her mobile on speakerphone. The ringing shrilled through the room.

The call picked up on the eighth ring. 'Hello?' said Jeremy Lightfoot. 'Sorry, the phone had slipped to the bottom of my bag.' Then a pause. 'Who is calling?'

'Oh hello, Jeremy,' said Pippa. 'It's Pippa Parker. We met in Much Gadding, at the literary festival meeting.'

'Oh yes, so we did,' said Jeremy. 'Look, I don't really have time to talk right now—'

'How's the study leave going?' asked Pippa.

'Oh, you know,' said Jeremy. 'Now, if this isn't urgent —'

'I wondered what you were doing last Friday morning,' said Pippa.

'Last Friday morning?' said Jeremy. 'Hold on, how did you get this number anyway? This is my personal mobile number.'

'I don't think you need to know that,' said Pippa. 'But I would like to know where you were and what you were doing on the morning of Friday the 29th, and I should probably inform you that I am liaising with the police about this matter. In fact, I have a police officer listening in right now.' Out of the corner of her eye, Pippa saw Jim put his head in his hands, and turned so that she couldn't see

160

him.

'I have absolutely no idea what you mean,' said Jeremy Lightfoot. 'Are you threatening me?'

'Not at all,' said Pippa. 'I just want you to answer my question. Where were you, and what were you doing last Friday morning?'

'I'm under no obligation to answer,' said Jeremy Lightfoot, 'but for the benefit of your police officer friend, I shall tell you that I was presenting a conference paper at the University of Bologna.'

'What?' said Pippa.

'I'm sure you heard me,' said Jeremy Lightfoot, his voice now silky-smooth. 'The sessions were all recorded, and I believe you can view them online if you go to the university website. I presented to an audience of four hundred people, and I'm sure that the conference organiser would be happy to confirm my attendance.' He paused. 'Mrs Parker, you mentioned that you have a police officer listening in. Would you mind putting him on the line?'

'I'm sure that won't be necessary,' gabbled Pippa.

'Oh, I think it is,' said Jeremy. 'I'd love to know what's been going on, and I have another twenty minutes until my flight is called. I feel it's only fair for me to know what you were trying to accuse me of.'

Pippa considered ending the call, but one look at Jim's face told her that would be a very bad idea. She passed her phone to him instead. 'I'll wait outside,' she muttered.

Only when she had closed the door of the police station behind her did Pippa allow herself to cry. 'What have I done?' she whispered, between sniffles.

Chapter 19

Pippa heard the creak of the police station door. Framed in the doorway was Jim Horsley, glaring at her. 'You owe me, Pippa,' he said. 'Big time.' He jerked his head towards the interior and Pippa, full of trepidation, followed him inside.

'Back room,' said Jim. He opened the door, and looked away as Pippa passed through. *It must be really bad.*

'Sit,' he said. 'You'll be glad to know that Jeremy Lightfoot isn't going to press charges against you. He did mention threats and intimidation, but I managed to talk him round.'

'Thank you,' croaked Pippa.

'I also managed not to tell him about this secret journal,' said Jim. 'However, in order to do that I had to tell him that those letters have gone missing.'

'Oh God,' said Pippa, and put her head in her hands.

'Mr Lightfoot wasn't happy that this has been kept under wraps, as you may imagine.'

'That wasn't me, that was Daphne—'

'I don't care who it was,' said Jim. 'The end result is

that these letters are still missing, and it appears as if we've been sitting on the matter. Which, in a way, we have. Anyway, Mr Lightfoot has asked to speak to Inspector Fanshawe, and I don't really have any choice other than to let him do that.' He paused. 'I told him that you were traumatised by the attempted break-in, and possibly had let it get to you a bit too much. Which I suspect is actually the case.' He studied Pippa. 'Would you like a cup of tea?'

'I want to dig a big hole, get in it, and pull it in after me,' said Pippa. 'What an absolute mess.' *And most of it's my own fault.* 'I'm sorry, Jim.'

Jim looked at the desk. 'It's OK,' he muttered. 'It'll probably blow over. We just need to get these damn letters back.'

'You won't get in trouble, will you?' Pippa's stomach churned in a most uncomfortable manner. 'I can phone the inspector and tell him it was nothing to do with you, and you were trying to stop me—'

Jim shrugged. 'We'll see,' he said.

'I'm sorry,' said Pippa, and as Jim still wasn't looking at her, she looked past him, and saw the time. 'Oh heck, I'd better go. It's time to fetch Ruby.'

The hint of a smile appeared on Jim's face. 'Yes, you do that, and have a quiet afternoon. And may I ask one thing?'

Pippa felt her cheeks flushing. 'Of course.'

'Stay out of this. For my sake, and your own.'

***

'Are you all right?' said Alicia, when she opened the nursery door. 'You look a bit peaky.'

'I might be coming down with something,' said Pippa. 'How has Ruby been?'

'Oh, fine,' said Alicia. 'She's learnt a lot of things in Cygnets, hasn't she?'

'Yes, she has,' said Pippa. 'That's why I was a bit surprised that you want to move her back.'

Alicia raised her carefully drawn eyebrows. 'It isn't up to me,' she said. 'She's still quite little, and you were worried she wouldn't cope—'

'I think kids are more resilient than we give them credit for,' said Pippa. 'At least, Ruby is.' *Maybe I can learn from her.*

'I'll just go and get her,' said Alicia. 'But if you don't mind me saying, Mrs Parker, you should go home and put your feet up. You really don't look well.'

'I've had better days, certainly,' said Pippa. But Alicia had already disappeared into the Duckling Room, and didn't hear.

'So how did you like being back with the Ducklings?' Pippa asked Ruby as they walked home.

Ruby screwed up her face. 'It was OK,' she said. 'But everyone's small.'

'Aren't you small any more, then?' asked Pippa.

Ruby considered the question. 'Bigger than small people. But smaller than big people,' she said. 'I don't know.'

'Mmm,' said Pippa. 'I don't think I know, either.'

'Can we have nice lunch, Mummy?' asked Ruby. 'Because I was with the small people?'

'Yes,' said Pippa. 'As long as there's something decent

to eat in the house. I'm too tired to go to the shops. I might be getting a cold.' *And I can't cope with any extra demands right now.*

***

At home she deployed the fairy DVD and put a pizza in the oven. Then she rang Briony, but the phone went to voicemail. 'It's Pippa. Call me when you're free, though I don't have good news for you,' she said, and hung up. *This will affect Briony too*, she thought. *Jeremy Lightfoot is bound to get access to the letters when they come back – assuming that they do come back...*

Could this be a smokescreen? He'll make a fuss about the letters, so that no one thinks he's got them—

Then she shook her head. 'Just stay out of it, Pippa,' she told herself. 'You've done enough damage already.' Then she thought of Daphne. *I must warn her. But how?*

In the end she texted Marge. *Could you give me Daphne's number, please? I need to tell her something.*

Marge sent the number a few minutes later. *Good luck with that*, she added. *She hasn't answered my calls for days. I don't know what's going on.*

Pippa shivered. The thought of telling Daphne what had happened was not pleasant. She was glad when the oven timer beeped, and she could put it off until after lunch.

In an attempt to save herself from even more guilt at parking her daughter in front of a DVD, Pippa asked Ruby to draw a picture of her favourite fairy, using the DVD case as inspiration. Having set her up at the dining-room table with plenty of paper and crayons, Pippa retreated to the kitchen and rang Daphne's number.

As she had expected, and hoped, it went to voicemail. 'Hello, this is Daphne Fairhurst. I can't take your call right now, but please leave a message and I shall return your call when I can.' A pause, and Pippa waited for the beep, but before it came she could just hear Daphne asking 'Do I press the button, Marge?' It almost made her burst into tears again.

'Hello, Daphne,' she said. 'It's Pippa Parker. I'm really sorry but I have bad news. I made a mistake, and now Jeremy Lightfoot knows that the letters are missing, and he is in touch with the police. I honestly didn't mean to do it —'

There was a scratching, fumbling noise, then a breathless 'Hello?'

Pippa's throat was so tight that she found it hard to speak. 'Hello, Daphne,' she croaked.

'I don't understand,' said Daphne. 'How did he—'

'I – I made a mistake,' said Pippa. 'Someone tried to break into my house, and the milkman saw someone hanging around who sounded like Jeremy Lightfoot, and I put two and two together, and I was wrong.'

'Someone tried to break into your house?' said Daphne. 'But why?'

'I thought they were after the journal,' said Pippa. 'I still have that safe, by the way.' She got up and went to her laptop bag to check that she was speaking the truth.

Daphne said nothing for at least a minute. 'I don't know what to say,' she said. 'I've been keeping this to myself for so many years, and now... I don't know what to do. I'd ask you to give the journal back to me, but...'

'I'm sorry,' said Pippa. 'Hopefully, with the police involved, they can find the letters.'

'It will never be the same,' said Daphne. 'And I'll never be allowed to forget it.' There was a quiet click, then the sound of a dead line.

Pippa went through to the kitchen and made herself a cup of tea. 'I'm not going to cry,' she told herself. 'There's no point in crying. It won't solve anything.' And as if by magic, her phone rang. *Briony*, said the display. Pippa swallowed and pressed *Accept*. *I might as well get it all over in one go.*

'Hello, Pippa,' said Briony. 'I take it no good news means bad news.'

'Yes,' said Pippa. 'Someone tried to break into my house while I was seeing you on Friday. For various reasons I won't go into, I was convinced it was Jeremy Lightfoot, so I got hold of his mobile number and found out that he was in Italy at the time. And now he knows that the letters have gone. Oh, and the police do too.'

Briony whistled. 'You don't do things by halves, do you?' A pause, during which Pippa could almost hear her brain whirring. 'What about the journal?'

'Luckily the policeman who dealt with Jeremy managed to keep that quiet,' said Pippa. 'But because of that, he had to tell Jeremy about the letters.' She sighed. 'I'm so sorry, Briony. I wanted you to get the chance to work on Clementina Stoate, not him.'

'It's OK,' said Briony. 'I've kind of got used to missed opportunities.'

'Please don't,' said Pippa. 'I can't handle any more

guilt.'

'You tried your best,' said Briony. 'We both did. But in the end, Jeremy won.'

'He hasn't won yet,' said Pippa. 'And we've still got the journal. For now, anyway. I told Daphne and she put the phone down on me.'

'Wow,' said Briony. 'That's pretty extreme for Daphne.'

'I know,' said Pippa. 'I feel awful.'

Briony sighed. 'I've got to go,' she said. 'I have a moderating meeting in five minutes. I'll keep going with what I've got, though. If you can, will you do the same?'

'I'll try,' said Pippa. 'Perhaps not today, though. Goodbye, Briony.'

***

Pippa kept herself busy for the rest of the afternoon supervising Ruby's drawing and colouring. Once they had collected Freddie, she set the children to junk modelling at the dining-room table while she started a ragu sauce for spaghetti bolognese. *I probably look like a model parent*, thought Pippa. *As if.*

She hoped Simon would be late, so that she could put off talking about her day, but he got home at half past five precisely. 'What happened to the traffic?' she said, trying not to sound resentful, as Simon took off his tie and hung it on the post at the bottom of the stairs.

'There wasn't much,' said Simon. 'What's for dinner?'

'Spag bol,' said Pippa. 'It's simmering now. I can put the spaghetti in whenever.'

Simon stared at her. 'From scratch? On a Monday?' Then he grinned. 'What have you been doing?'

'Oh don't,' said Pippa. 'I've had a terrible day.'

'Do you want to talk about it?' Simon studied her. 'Later, maybe?'

Pippa nodded, not trusting herself to speak.

'Shall I go and talk to the kids for a bit?' She nodded again, and Simon disappeared. Presently she heard them laughing, and went back into the kitchen, too depressed to join them.

After dinner, Simon volunteered to get the children ready for bed. 'You've had them all day,' he said, 'it's only fair. Why don't you go and sit down? Watch telly, or something.'

Pippa went into the sitting room, switched on the TV, and stared at the screen. She watched a trailer for a new drama series, and then the title sequence for *Gadcestershire Today* began, with the presenter's familiar voice announcing the items over the top. 'A literary treasure hunt: Jeremy Lightfoot calls on Gadcestershire residents to help track down some very important letters.'

Pippa stared at the screen. 'Am I going mad?' she asked herself. She turned the volume up, then went into the kitchen and made herself a strong cup of tea. She was just pouring in the milk when she heard Jeremy Lightfoot's voice, and hurried back into the sitting room.

'These letters are of vital importance,' said Jeremy Lightfoot, in a room lined with books. 'They have been hidden away for decades, and are likely to be full of literary gems. And now that they have gone missing we must find them. I call upon everyone in Gadcestershire to look out for the letters. They were in a black folder when they went missing, and they were written by Clementina Stoate, a notable Victorian poet.' He gazed into the camera. 'If you have seen letters like these, or if you have perhaps found them, please return them to your local police station. You will not get in trouble, for I have secured an amnesty. The important thing is that we secure them for the nation. Please help us to maintain Gadcestershire's literary heritage.'

'Jeremy Lightfoot speaking there,' said the presenter. 'As he said, please get in touch with your local police station if you have seen or know anything about the letters. Here is the number to call. You will be charged at the local rate.'

Pippa sipped her tea without thinking, and gasped as she scalded her mouth. *It's probably the right thing to do*, she thought. *Perhaps it's what we should have done in the first place.* She blinked, and a tear rolled down her face. She let it drip into her mug. It really didn't seem to matter.

Chapter 20

'Pippa. *Pippa.*'

Pippa felt someone shaking her gently, and opened an eye. 'Not time to get up yet,' she murmured, and turned over.

'You don't have to get up,' said Simon. 'You don't even have to open your eyes. Just listen to the radio.'

Pippa groaned, freed an ear from the duvet, and tried to focus on the voice of Dave Bassett, the local news reporter.

'The letters were found by Fred Carter, a local resident, while walking his dog early this morning. Mr Carter spotted the file in the church porch, and recognised it from the description which Jeremy Lightfoot, the well-known author and television presenter, gave on *Gadcestershire Today* yesterday evening. We understand the owner of the letters is delighted to have them back.'

'All's well that ends well, eh,' said Ritz Robertson. 'It shows that when you get the public involved, things happen. Well done to Jeremy Lightfoot, I say. And speaking of Jeremy Lightfoot, we'll be hearing from him later on today's programme. Here's a bit of appropriate music.' Pippa recognised the introduction to Alison Moyet's cover of 'Love Letters'.

'There you go,' said Simon. 'The letters have been found. Hopefully everyone can forget it and get on with their lives. Including Jeremy Lightfoot.' He leaned over and kissed her. 'I'll get the kettle on.'

I want to feel relieved, thought Pippa, staring at the ceiling. *I ought to be happy that the letters have turned up, and Daphne has them back.* She sighed. *There's bound to be an event now, with all the media interest that Jeremy Lightfoot has whipped up.* She smiled wryly. *Fair play to him, he's got the most out of it.* Then a thought struck her. *I wonder where he is?*

She reached for her phone, and searched for Jeremy's website. It had a tab for events, and she noted that today he was speaking at a Robert Louis Stevenson symposium in Edinburgh. She checked his biography, which said that he lived in York with his family. Thinking about it, the setting he had appeared in the previous evening definitely had the air of a home office or study. Much as she would like to pin the theft of the letters on Jeremy Lightfoot, it seemed extremely improbable that he could have flown from Bologna to England, been filmed at home in York in the late afternoon or early evening, popped down to Much Gadding to drop off the file of letters, and got himself up to Edinburgh for a conference.

The last piano notes of 'Love Letters' faded away, and she tuned back into the radio.

'And now we have Jeremy Lightfoot on the line,' said

Ritz. 'You must be delighted with the success of your campaign, Jeremy.'

'Yes, I certainly am,' said Jeremy. 'Please excuse any background noise, I'm in a hotel on the Royal Mile in Edinburgh, and the bagpipers are already out in force.' Indeed, Pippa could hear a faint droning and whining underpinning Jeremy's smooth tones.

'Excellent, excellent,' said Ritz.

'What is fascinating about the letters,' said Jeremy, 'is actually how few of them have been published. Clementina Stoate is, in my view, an unjustly neglected poet who ought to be a national treasure. I am hoping to secure an opportunity to publish her collected poems and letters, so that Victorian scholars can access Clementina's work on an equitable basis. The time has passed for important manuscripts to be squirrelled away and made inaccessible. Openness is the key. In fact, I am hoping to organise a literary event featuring the works of Clementina Stoate in Much Gadding this summer.'

'Oh, really?' said Ritz.

'Indeed, yes,' said Jeremy. 'It will be aimed at the general reader, rather than academics and scholars, and I hope there will be something interesting and enjoyable for everyone.'

'You heard it here first,' said Ritz Robertson. 'Lovely to talk to you, Jeremy.'

'And you too, Rich,' said Jeremy.

Well, that's one event I won't be involved with, thought Pippa. *I've burnt my boats there, and no mistake.*

'Here you go,' said Simon, handing her a cup of tea.

'Do you feel better now?'

'Not particularly,' said Pippa. 'I think I've committed career suicide. Jeremy Lightfoot won't want me anywhere near his festival, and I've let my paid work slide as well.' She shrugged. 'I'll just have to apologise to all my clients and get back on the case this afternoon.'

Simon stared at her. 'You do realise most of them won't even have noticed?' he said. 'Serendipity's still on her book tour, you said the other day that you've got the Proms in hand, the holiday lets don't kick off until summer anyway, and you've sorted out a new residency for Jeff and the group.'

'I suppose,' said Pippa. 'But I haven't given it my full attention, and that needs to stop.' She drank her tea, looking at nothing in particular. 'Playgroup will probably be full of it this morning.'

'Doesn't matter,' said Simon. 'They didn't know you were searching for the letters anyway. Let them gossip.'

'I just wonder...' said Pippa. *Who had the letters?* It wasn't Jeremy Lightfoot; that was obvious now. There was no way he could have got them to Much Gadding overnight.

Her mind ranged through the people who had come to Daphne's house that evening. Malcolm and Norm she had discounted. Lady Higginbotham... Pippa shook her head. She wouldn't have made a midnight excursion to the church porch, and Beryl wouldn't have agreed to it, either. Jeremy Lightfoot, sadly, was out of the running. *That leaves Marge*, Pippa thought, and her heart sank. She remembered the drawer at Marge's house which she hadn't been able to open. Perhaps the file had been there all along. Or she could have given it to Briony, who had kept it secret, then returned it when Jeremy Lightfoot made his appeal.

But that doesn't make sense, thought Pippa. *Why would she give the letters back the moment they were asked for?* She recalled her meeting with Briony. *I don't believe that she lied to me. And if she didn't have the letters, what would be the point in Marge taking them?*

On impulse, she texted Marge. *Have you heard on the radio? Daphne's letters have been found.*

A reply came after a few minutes. *Didn't know they'd gone missing. I've just been reading about it on the Chronicle website. Internet's rubbish here.*

Why, where are you? Pippa replied.

Centre Parcs in Sherwood Forest. Nephew got a good deal and I've been roped in for babysitting. Didn't I say?

I must have missed it, Pippa typed. She added *Have fun!* and pressed *Send*. Relief washed over her. *It wasn't Marge. I knew it couldn't be.*

But who was it? Who could have taken the letters, then left them in the church porch in the dead of night?

It can't be a random person, she thought. *They would have taken the letters to the police station. It was someone who didn't want to get caught.* She flipped through her list of suspects, her brain working through the possibilities. Suddenly, a glimmer of light.

'Ahhh,' she said, and finished her tea.

'That sounds significant,' said Simon. 'Care to share?'

'I've already got myself into quite enough trouble by

sharing,' said Pippa. 'I'm going to think this through carefully before I do anything at all.'

Simon snorted. 'Mystery woman,' he said, and drained his mug. 'Well, some of us have got to go to work. I'll leave you to your significant thoughts.'

***

Despite impeccable behaviour from Ruby at playgroup, and lunch without tears, the morning had dragged. Pippa had reached her conclusion, thought through the idea from all angles, and, confident that she had at last got it right, only wanted the opportunity to test her theory.

'Someone's got plans,' said Sheila, when Pippa dropped Ruby off for the afternoon.

'Oh, this and that,' said Pippa. 'Plenty of work to do.'

'You aren't normally this eager about work, though,' said Sheila. 'I shall wait to hear.'

'Mmm,' said Pippa. 'If I'm right, my plan is that you won't ever hear.'

'Should I be worried?' Sheila gave her a suspicious look.

'Not this time,' said Pippa. 'I'll definitely be back by three.'

She drove home, checked she was neat and tidy, and set out on the short walk into the village. She had a call to make.

Pippa knocked, and waited. After a minute she heard a bolt rattle. Presently the door opened a tiny bit, and Daphne peered through the gap, just above the chain. 'Oh,' she said, when she saw Pippa.

'Hello, Daphne,' said Pippa. 'You must be very glad to

have the letters back.'

'Oh yes,' said Daphne. 'Yes, I am. Very glad.' She peered at Pippa. 'Did you want to speak to me?'

'Yes, I do,' said Pippa. 'Is that OK? I mean, you've got the letters now.'

'Yes,' said Daphne. 'The vicar brought them round early this morning. I've put them away in Clementina's desk. Wait a moment.' The door closed while the chain was taken off, then reopened. 'You may come in for a few minutes, if you like.'

'Thank you,' said Pippa. 'I won't be long.'

Daphne's sitting room was exactly the same. Somehow Pippa had expected it to be different: disordered, or untidy. 'Have you decided what to do about the letters?' she asked.

Daphne sat opposite Pippa; her shoulders hunched, her whole body tense. 'Not yet. I understand Jeremy Lightfoot has mentioned – publication.'

'He has, yes,' said Pippa. 'That's exactly what you didn't want, isn't it?'

Daphne looked uncomfortable. 'I just don't feel it's right to publish people's private letters,' she said. 'I mean, Clementina never knew that would happen when she wrote them.'

'No,' said Pippa. 'I should have realised that when the letters went missing.'

Daphne shot a quick, birdlike glance at her. 'What do you mean?'

'It seemed so obvious that Jeremy Lightfoot had taken them,' said Pippa. 'He had the motive, he was the only person carrying a large bag, and he made sure nobody could get hold of him. But thinking about it, even with all the fuss over his laptop, it would have been extremely difficult for him to sneak that file into his bag.'

'I don't understand,' said Daphne.

'The file was too big for anyone to take it that evening without being seen,' said Pippa. 'One by one, I discounted everybody. Nobody had both the motivation and the opportunity to do it.' She looked at Daphne. 'So that leaves you. You didn't want a big fuss over the letters, or about Clementina Stoate at all. So it made much more sense to tell me the letters were gone, refuse to report it to the police, and let me investigate, knowing that you had the letters safely tucked away. If nothing else, it would give you a breathing space.'

Daphne kept her eyes fixed on Pippa, but said nothing.

'When Jeremy Lightfoot heard the letters were missing and got the police involved, you knew you had to act. Luckily, Jeremy suggested an amnesty. People were told to take the letters to the police station, but instead they turned up at the church porch. And you are the one person in the village who couldn't arrive with the letters and say you'd found them somewhere. The fact that you took the letters to the church that same night suggests to me that you wanted the fuss over as quickly as possible.' Pippa paused. 'I could point out that your shoes, by the front door, have mud and grass on the soles, that the path to the churchyard is overgrown and muddy, and that it rained yesterday evening. But I don't think I need to.'

'I'm sorry,' said Daphne. 'I'm sorry that I let you investigate. I should never have done it. I just wanted it all to stop.' She looked at Pippa with wet eyes. 'Did you get in trouble?'

Pippa smiled. 'A bit. But I imagine it'll blow over. These things usually do.'

Daphne sniffed. 'I thought I was doing the right thing, and I've made such a mess.' A slow tear ran down her cheek. 'What happens now?' she whispered.

Chapter 21

'This is amazing,' said Briony, for perhaps the fifth time.

'What, my dining room?' said Pippa.

Briony snorted. 'You know what I mean. I've never had exclusive access to anything before.'

'Don't get too used to it,' said Pippa. 'Daphne said that we can have a week, then she'll decide what to do. So we'd better get on with it.'

'Yes, boss,' said Briony, and turned over another page in the black file.

'Apart from anything else,' said Pippa, 'I'll have to go and fetch Freddie at three o'clock. Ruby is in her Wednesday afternoon session, so I can get her later, but we'll have a five-year-old to deal with.'

'He'll probably behave better than some of my students,' said Briony.

'Don't be too sure,' said Pippa.

They had been reading, and pondering, and not speaking much for the last hour. Occasionally Pippa scribbled a note, but she didn't feel she was getting far.

'Look,' she said, 'what do you think?'

Briony pushed the file gently away and tapped her teeth with one of the pencils she had insisted they both use. 'I don't know,' she said. 'The gaps are the problem. Clementina must have been very busy once she got more famous, and that means her letters are shorter, the journal entries are shorter, there aren't as many… It's so hard to know what really happened.'

'Let's look at the poems again,' said Pippa.

'It feels as if we're going round in circles,' said Briony. 'It's so unfair that we only have a week.'

'But we *have* a week,' said Pippa, 'and we can't waste the opportunity.'

'I know,' said Briony. 'Do you want to take the book, or the handwritten poems?'

'I don't mind,' said Pippa. 'You choose.'

'I'll have the book,' said Briony. 'I need a break from her handwriting.'

She handed the black file carefully to Pippa, and Pippa leafed through the plastic wallets. She hadn't realised until she had received the file from Daphne that there were some handwritten copies of poems at the end. 'You never mentioned these,' she had said.

'I didn't think they were important,' said Daphne. 'I know they're in Clementina's handwriting, but they must be fair copies.'

Pippa read an early poem about a marble statue in Gadcester Museum. She didn't enjoy it. Then she turned to 'Daisies at Dawn', written many years later. It was an easy, charming read, but behind it lurked something else.

Something menacing. And then she found the last poem, 'The Key', which was as convoluted and baffling as the first.

'I just don't get it,' she said.

Briony glanced up from her book. 'What don't you get?'

'I know I'm an amateur,' said Pippa. 'But I did English A-level and we had to do poetry, which involves reading a lot of poems by the same person. And even if they were a bit different, you could always tell it was them.' She looked at Briony. 'Will you humour me for a moment? Well, maybe five minutes.'

Briony sighed. 'Might as well. I'm getting nowhere.'

'OK.' Pippa tore out two pages of her notebook. 'Will you copy out "The Rabbit" for me, then on another page, a verse or two of any of the early ones?'

Briony raised an eyebrow. 'Have I been naughty in class? Is that why you're making me copy out poems?'

'I'll make a cup of tea afterwards,' said Pippa. 'Look, I'm doing it too.' She flicked through the plastic wallets, and quickly wrote out 'Daisies at Dawn', and on a separate sheet, two verses of a poem about a naiad living in the River Gad.

'OK, done,' said Briony. 'Can I have a biscuit, now I've been good?'

'Hold your horses,' said Pippa. 'This is just an experiment, and I could be barking up the wrong tree, but —' She put her copy of 'Daisies at Dawn' in the centre of the table between them. 'Can you put your copy of "The Rabbit" next to it, then look at them both together.'

Briony put her sheet beside Pippa's, and stared at them. 'What am I looking for?'

'Tell me what you see.'

'I see two poems by Clementina Stoate.'

'Even though they're in different handwriting?'

'Yep.' Briony glanced at Pippa. 'I'm quite thirsty, you know.'

'OK, bear with me.' Pippa moved the sheets aside. 'Now, put the other poem you chose in the middle of the table.'

Briony did so, and Pippa added the naiad poem. 'Can you tell me what you see, please.'

Briony shrugged. 'Two poems by Clementina Stoate.'

Pippa took back the poem Briony had chosen, and substituted 'The Rabbit'. 'Now look, and tell me what you see.'

'I see...' She peered at the sheets, then picked them both up and studied them. Then she looked at Pippa. 'It's probably because they're in different handwriting,' she said.

'OK, try this.' Pippa took away 'The Rabbit' and substituted 'Daisies at Dawn'. 'Now you have two poems in the same handwriting. What do you see?'

Briony examined both poems. 'Your handwriting isn't very neat,' she said.

'Stop playing for time,' said Pippa.

'I see two poems,' said Briony. 'Two poems in the same handwriting, but different in style, syntax, vocabulary, rhythm, and treatment of the subject matter. And if these weren't in the same handwriting, I would never have thought they were written by the same person.'

She stared at Pippa, then put the poems down and grabbed the pair in her own handwriting. 'And with these . . . I see exactly the same thing. Two poems that I don't believe are written by the same person.' She met Pippa's eyes. 'Oh my God.'

'That's the thing I've never been able to get into my head,' said Pippa. 'The poems people know, the ones that you come across in anthologies, are nothing like the ones Clementina wrote before. The only later one anything like those is "The Key". And nobody knows what that's about anyway.' She thought back to the previous day, when she had finally worked out the conundrum of who had taken the letters. 'I should have known. It was the simplest answer, and because it seemed so impossible we just ignored it.'

'But if Clementina didn't write these,' said Briony, 'then who did?'

'It must have been someone close to her,' said Pippa, 'and someone who could read and write, obviously.'

'Her husband Charles would be the obvious person,' said Briony. 'He could certainly write. And Clementina's poetic output ended when he died—'

'But from what I remember,' said Pippa, 'she never mentioned that Charles had any literary ambitions.'

'Well, she wouldn't, would she?' said Briony. 'Not if she was going to pinch his poetry.'

'But why would he let her?' said Pippa. 'I mean, he clearly knew she was growing much more famous, and he would have seen the magazines she was published in.'

'Unless he wanted to keep his authorship quiet,' said Briony. 'Maybe he thought it would detract from his business.'

'But I thought it normally worked the other way round,' said Pippa. 'Like George Eliot and the Brontës, publishing under male names.'

'Yes, but if Clementina was hungry for success, then maybe Charles let her have the poems out of kindness,' said Briony.

'Wouldn't that be awful, though,' said Pippa. 'You've been trying all these years to become a famous poet, and then your husband writes a few poems, drops them into your lap, and says, "Here you go".'

Briony laughed. 'I'm not sure it was exactly like that, Pippa. But you must admit it's an interesting hypothesis.'

'It is,' said Pippa. 'But to quote you from whenever it was, is there any evidence to back it up?' She thought for a moment. 'Hang on, Clementina did use a pen name. You remember, when she submitted those first poems to Mr Chapman.'

Briony smiled. 'You do realise you're turning into a Clementina Stoate expert.' She picked up the book again. 'Here it is. Miss M. Wright.'

'But why bother?' said Pippa. 'If she knew the poems were good – I mean really good, better than her other work – why did she use a pen name? And why submit to a different magazine? Surely it would make more sense to send them somewhere she was known.'

'Mmm,' said Briony. 'You have a point there.' She frowned. 'Another thing is that usually a pen name has some sort of relevance. "George Eliot" is related to Marian Evans's lover, and the Brontës used ambiguous first names with the same initial as their own names. So why is M. Wright significant?'

'M,' said Pippa. 'M for Mary. She could write. She went for walks in the countryside, and she would have seen the things in these poems. We need to find out her surname, but I don't think it's mentioned anywhere in the letters.'

'I think you're jumping to conclusions,' said Briony. 'I agree there is some evidence, but...' Pippa could almost see the lightbulb glow above her head. 'The census!' she cried. 'We can check the census online. That will tell us the names of everyone under the Stoates' roof. If only it's close enough.'

'I don't think it will be,' said Pippa. 'The closest would be in 1881, when Mary was already dead.'

'Damn,' said Briony softly. 'Just when I thought we were getting somewhere.'

'There are other records,' said Pippa. 'Parish records, death records...' She opened her laptop. 'Let's try the Ancestry website.' She found the site, and began clicking. 'Briony, can you find me the date of Mary's death.'

'July 24, 1878,' Briony replied. 'No, wait – that's when she was found. So the day before.' She moved her chair closer to Pippa's.

'In the parish of Much Gadding.' Pippa typed rapidly. 'Here goes nothing.'

They watched the screen. *Searching...*

Both jumped when the record appeared.

Mary Wright, aged 19. Date death registered: 24th July 1878. Parish: Much Gadding. District: Gadcestershire.

'It can't be a coincidence,' muttered Briony. 'It just can't.'

'We need the full certificate,' said Pippa. 'That will give us Mary Wright's occupation, and where she lived, and the informant. But I'd be prepared to bet right now that this Mary and our Mary are one and the same.'

'Mary Wright,' said Briony. 'Mary Wright.' Her voice cracked on the last word. 'Clementina hated her. Clementina thwarted her. Clementina went to her room and took her letters and her magazines, and burned them.' She opened Clementina's journal and found the entry. '*Her bedside table was littered with cheap magazines and pieces of paper covered in scribbles. Letters...*' Her voice tailed off. 'Letters and magazines, and she put them in the fire. Magazines, yes, but who would have lots of letters they had written scattered over their bedside table?'

'Pieces of paper with Mary's handwriting on,' said Pippa. 'Clementina wrote in her journal that they were letters. She would tell Charles that they were letters. But she didn't burn them, did she? And when she had put the magazines in the fire, she took Mary's writings to her room and began, she writes, composing a poem. And shortly afterwards she sent two poems to Mr Chapman, under Mary's name.'

'Circumstantially, it's all there,' said Briony. 'But how do we prove it? How on earth do we prove it?'

They both jumped as Pippa's alarm shrilled. 'I hate to tell you this,' said Pippa, 'but it's time I went to get

Freddie. I'll be gone twenty, maybe thirty minutes, and I can't guarantee how much attention I'll be able to give this afterwards.'

'It's OK,' said Briony. 'To be honest, I'm exhausted. I never expected this. I never expected anything like this.' She sighed. 'And I have a pile of marking to do, and no more free time until Friday afternoon.'

'Come back then,' said Pippa. 'I'll switch Ruby's nursery sessions. Stay over, if you need to. But we have to work this out. We can't let it go.'

She thought of Mary returning from church that day, possibly full of religious fervour, perhaps glad to have got through a boring service, and going to her room to find her poems vanished, and as the mistress of the house would have informed her, burnt. 'I have no idea what Daphne will say, but we have to do this. For Mary.'

Chapter 22

Oh no, thought Pippa, as Lila strode across the playground with a distinct gleam in her eye. She bent and scooped Ruby into her arms.

'Mummy!' Ruby wriggled. 'I'm too big!'

'What, you mean you don't want to cuddle?' said Pippa.

'Not now, Mummy!' Ruby wriggled some more.

'All right,' said Pippa. She lowered Ruby to the ground, but kept hold of her hand.

'Can I have a quick word?' Lila asked. From her expression, which was businesslike, it didn't look as if it would be quick.

'What about?' asked Pippa.

'Work stuff,' said Lila. 'Your work stuff.'

'Could we do it another time?' Pippa's grip on Ruby's hand tightened a little. 'As you can see I've got Ruby with me, and I don't think the playground is the best place for this sort of conversation.'

'Fine,' said Lila, stepping back and folding her arms. 'I'll text you.'

'OK,' said Pippa. 'We can talk later, maybe.'

'Yes, maybe,' said Lila. 'Catch you later.' And she walked away, heading for the line forming outside the classroom.

Crisis averted, thought Pippa. *I can't handle anything else right now.*

'Can I do letters?' asked Ruby, as they walked home.

'I don't see why not,' said Pippa. 'You can sit at the dining-room table with me while I work, if you like.'

Pippa set Ruby up with lined paper and a pencil, and herself with a cup of tea. As she had expected, Lila's text wasn't long in coming.

I expect you've seen Jeff's email.

Oh, good grief. Pippa opened her laptop and checked her email. Near the top was one from Jeff, dated yesterday, 8.30 pm.

Hi Pippa,

I'd like your opinion, and I thought I'd email as this is too long for a text.

I had a call from Jed James earlier today. He's really pleased with how the residency is going, and as you know we're doing six weeks. It turns out that there's another Rumours in Mumford, which his cousin manages, and Jed asked if we'd like him to have a word with his cousin about a follow-on residency there.

My initial reaction is yes, great, and Lewis and the lads agree, but Lila isn't so sure. We had a chat last night, and she thinks I should ask your opinion.

So I'm asking. What do you think?

Kind regards,
Jeff

Pippa sighed, and picked up her phone. *Yes, I've seen it,* she replied.

And...?

Give me a chance, thought Pippa. *Well, I'll check out the nightclub, of course,* she texted. *But yes, I think it's a brilliant opportunity.*

Well I don't, and I want you to back me up.

Pippa put her phone on the table and ran her hands through her hair in frustration, then picked up the phone again. *Is this about you know what?*

Of course it is. This is exactly what I didn't want to happen. You're my friend, and I need your help.

Pippa counted to ten before hitting *Reply*. *Of course I'm your friend, Lila. But Jeff is my client, and I can't give him bad advice.*

The reply came in seconds: *Some friend you are.*

Lila clearly hadn't counted to ten. Pippa put her phone face down, leaned back in her chair, closed her eyes, and took a deep breath.

'Are you sleeping, Mummy?' asked Ruby.

Pippa looked at her daughter. 'No, Ruby. It's – something difficult at work.'

'Work's difficult,' said Ruby. 'Speshy K.'

Pippa scrutinised Ruby's sheet of paper, which now showed a wiggly line of mutilated half-butterflies. 'It shouldn't be, though,' she said. 'Not if you like your job. And mostly, I do.' She picked up her phone. 'Thanks,

Ruby.'

'You're welcome,' said Ruby, and, her tongue protruding, began another downstroke.

Pippa's thumbs flew over the keyboard. *Lila, you asked me to manage Jeff because of the conflict of interest between you managing him and personal stuff. I don't want to lose you as a friend, and I'd like to keep Jeff as a client, but if one of those has to go, then it's Jeff.* She pressed *Send*, then continued. *I can tell Jeff I'm very busy, which is true. But this problem will recur, whoever manages Jeff, until you tell him how you feel.*

This time there was a gap of several minutes before Lila's reply. *Jeff can do gigs in the back of beyond any old time. My time is running out. Don't you understand?*

Pippa considered what to reply. *Yes, but does Jeff?* She paused, thinking, then pressed *Send*. Then she looked at the time, and pressed *Reply* again. *I'm leaving for playgroup soon, but you can still text me. I won't reply to Jeff yet. But I really think you should talk. Honestly.*

'I've done my best,' she said, and closed the laptop. 'Come along Ruby, time for shoes.'

Ruby trotted into the hall and sat expectantly on the lowest step of the staircase. 'Wait a minute,' said Pippa. 'If you're too big to be picked up in the playground, aren't you big enough to put your own shoes on?'

Ruby gazed up at her. 'This is home,' she said, 'not the playground.'

***

Pippa had just sat down after putting out all the toys at playgroup when she felt her phone buzz. *Great timing,*

Lila, she thought, digging it out of her pocket. *Why would you even think of calling me at playgroup?* But when she looked at the display, it said *Much Gadding Police.*

'Hello?' said Pippa.

'Hello, Mrs Parker,' said PC Gannet, sounding perhaps more cheery than she had ever heard him before. 'Just calling with an update. We've apprehended the person who attempted to break into your house.'

'Oh, really?' said Pippa. 'Who was it?' *I suppose it's too much to hope it was Jeremy Lightfoot*, she thought.

'It was a young lad from Lower Gadding,' said PC Gannet. 'He got caught when he actually managed to break into someone's house, using the same method as he did at yours. Unfortunately for him the owner of the house was a ju-jitsu expert, and when I arrived at the house I found the perpetrator practically tied up in a knot. I took him to the station, and after a brief interview he confessed to attempting to break into several properties, including yours. I think he's learnt his lesson.'

'So that's that then,' said Pippa.

'Excuse me?' said PC Gannet.

'I mean, that's wonderful news,' said Pippa. 'Thank you very much for ringing to tell me. I do appreciate it.'

'Just doing my duty, ma'am,' said PC Gannet, and Pippa could picture him adjusting his cap as he said it. 'I'll let you get on.'

Pippa watched Ruby turning the pages of a board book, and pondered. *Poor Lila. I wish she'd tell him. I'm sure Jeff would understand.* Then her phone buzzed again. Pippa braced herself, and looked.

Serendipity: *Last stop on the book tour today, back sometime tomorrow. Fancy a coffee and a catch-up?*

Pippa smiled. *That would be great*, she replied. *Let me know when you've recovered!* Then she opened her notes app and added *Check S website stats and social media feeds* to her task list. *I bet she's gained loads of followers.*

She imagined Serendipity being interviewed, smiling shyly at her audience, signing piles of books and chatting to people. *I wonder what a Victorian salon was like. I doubt Clementina Stoate sat there and signed poetry books.* But it had been fame, of a kind. And while Clementina had hinted at reluctance in her journal, that didn't mean she wasn't ready to embrace it fully. *I bet she loved it*, thought Pippa. *Doing readings and discussing her work. And the poems people really wanted to hear, and hear about, weren't even hers.*

Then she recalled Lila's last words to her. *My time is running out. Don't you understand?*

That's it, thought Pippa. *Clementina's time was running out. Not in the same sense as Lila; but she had tried her hardest to become a successful, respected poet, and while she had minor success, it wasn't on the scale she wanted. So when she found Mary's poems, she grabbed the chance with both hands.*

But then Mary died.

Why? She was young, presumably healthy—

Pippa saw Clementina's regular, flawless writing in her mind's eye. *Clementina wrote that she was probably pregnant.*

Clementina wrote lots of things. But I'm coming to see

that many of them weren't true.

'I need a cup of tea,' said Pippa, to nobody in particular. 'Can someone watch Ruby for a few minutes?'

She got up, went to the kitchen, and fetched a cup and saucer from the cupboard. The urn had been filled, and she switched it on.

Mary drowned, and they found no marks of violence. But they wouldn't have examined her closely, and they wouldn't have been able to find out half as much as we would today. She wasn't visibly hurt before she went into the river, but that doesn't mean someone couldn't have drowned her. And if she was approached by someone she knew, she wouldn't have worried...

The urn grumbled at Pippa.

But why? Mary wrote the poems that Clementina stole and passed off as her own. Why kill the goose that laid the golden eggs?

Pippa dropped a teabag into her cup.

There's only one possible reason. Mary had found Clementina out, and would expose her. And that was enough for Clementina to kill her—

She jumped at a cough in the doorway. 'Sorry,' said Caitlin. 'Did I scare you?'

'Just thinking about something,' said Pippa. 'I was miles away.'

'I can see that,' said Caitlin. 'Through there, they were thinking of sending out a search party. Anyway, are you making that tea, or what? I'm dying for a cup.'

'Very funny,' said Pippa.

Chapter 23

'Guess what I found,' said Briony, when Pippa opened the front door.

Pippa studied her. 'The way things are, it could be anything, Briony. Clementina Stoate's long-lost daughter? Charles's secret diaries?'

'It isn't quite as good as either of those things,' said Briony, looking rather deflated. 'But I found the online archive for what was Gadcester Workhouse. And they've digitised lots of the records.'

'Ahh,' said Pippa. 'Victorian records?'

'You bet,' said Briony. 'Now if you'll let me in, I'll show you.'

In the end it was easy to swap Ruby's Friday session from morning to afternoon. 'Not a problem,' said Mrs Snell, on the phone. 'Not now that she's in Cygnets.'

'And will you keep her there?' said Pippa.

Mrs Snell considered. 'I don't see why not,' she said. 'She's adjusted very well. And she'd be cross if we put her back in Ducklings.'

'You're probably right,' said Pippa. 'It's amazing what we can do when we're given the opportunity.'

'Excuse me?' said Mrs Snell.

'Oh, nothing,' said Pippa. 'Just thinking aloud.'

So she had taken Ruby to nursery in very good time indeed, and then sat at the dining-room table, black file open, journal at the ready, and a blank page of her notebook to hand, and fidgeted until Briony rang the doorbell.

'Most of it's pretty run-of-the-mill,' said Briony. 'Daily timetables, the menu – not that there's much variety in that – accounts of visits from worthies in the parish. But then there's this.' She opened her laptop, unlocked it, and clicked on one of the minimised windows. 'This is the punishment book.'

'The punishment book?' Pippa leaned forward. The layout reminded her of Norm's library ledger, except considerably more ominous. Not to mention indecipherable.

'It is a bit tough to read,' said Briony. 'But look here.' She moved the cursor and pointed.

Mary Wright, aged 10. Misdemeanour: Daydreaming in lessons. Punishment: bread and water for dinner.

'She's in there a lot,' said Briony. 'She sounds like a handful. So far I've found her playing a prank on another girl, failing to pay attention – several times – and also telling stories to the other children after lights out. Oh yes, and there's one other thing.' She cast a sidelong glance at

Pippa.

'Go on,' said Pippa.

'Pinching stationery,' said Briony. 'She was writing even then. Look.' She scrolled down.

Misdemeanour: Pencil and several sheets of paper discovered under the mattress. Punishment: slipper.

'How I wish we knew more about Mary,' said Pippa. 'It's terrible that all we'll ever know is through other people's words. And frankly, I know more than I want to about Clementina Stoate.'

'But still not enough,' said Briony. 'Not enough to prove it. And we've gone through everything, I'm sure we have.'

'Everything became so sparse once she grew famous,' said Pippa. 'And now we have a good idea why. I'm prepared to bet that none of those later poems were hers.'

'Mmm,' said Briony. 'With one exception. Don't forget "The Key".'

Pippa shrugged. 'But no one understands it. That's the only reason it got included in the *Selected Poems*. No one's got a clue what it's about.' She pushed her fringe off her forehead. 'Anyway, I'm putting the kettle on. Tea? Coffee?'

'Black coffee please,' said Briony. 'Strong. I've been teaching the eighteenth century this morning, and I'll be glad when it's the weekend.'

When Pippa came back in with the drinks, she found Briony reading the *Selected Poems*. 'Anything?' she said, setting Briony's mug down. 'I made it double strength.'

'Cheers.' They clinked mugs, and Pippa glanced over Briony's shoulder.

There is a key within a key
And therein lies a mystery.
Framed in oak and bound in willow,
Prisoned, fated ne'er to grow.

'I mean, what is this?' she said.

Two pairs of hands have forged this key;
Two hearts devoured by enmity,
But joined withal in mutual passion.
Dedicated so to fashion

Broideries of tales not told,
Threads of silver, threads of gold.
Treasures which are locked away,
Ever deathless, past decay.

Washed by time, our lives will fade,
Step from sunshine into shade.
If you wish the truth to see—
All that's needed is the key.

Pippa shook her head. 'I feel as if I ought to understand it.'

'Well, we can guess who the two pairs of hands belong to now,' said Briony. 'Most academics thought Clementina was talking about her relationship with Charles. But I think she means Mary.'

'But they didn't work together,' said Pippa. 'How can stealing someone's poems be a key?'

'I don't know,' said Briony. 'I'd have to get into Clementina's head. And to be honest, I'd really rather not.' She sipped her coffee and her shoulders jerked a fraction.

Pippa opened the other copy of the *Selected Poems* and turned to 'The Key'. She imagined Clementina sitting at her desk, trying to summon a poem. 'Framed in oak? How the heck can you frame a key?'

'Search me,' said Briony. 'Unless you put it in a picture frame. You see those sometimes, don't you? Collections of keys in frames, in antique shops.'

'You do,' said Pippa, 'but I don't think that's it.' She closed her eyes and visualised Clementina, sitting there with a plentiful supply of paper, pens, ink, and everything she could want. Except inspiration. Looking around the room, looking out of the window—

The window.

'I think she was looking out of the window,' she said. 'In her study. That would have a wooden frame.'

'She might have been,' said Briony, without interest.

'I don't know if it's the same room,' said Pippa. 'Briony, can you go through the journal and check for references to a willow tree near the house? I'll phone Daphne.'

'So you think it's an actual tree?' said Briony. 'Not a symbol?' But Pippa had stopped listening.

As she had expected, Daphne's phone went to voicemail. 'Daphne, it's Pippa. I have a question, and it's urgent. Could you tell me if Clementina's desk is in the room she used as a study? If you can call me back—'

A click, and some scrabbling. 'Hello? Hello? Did I get it in time?' said Daphne.

'Hello, Daphne,' said Pippa. 'Did you hear my message?'

'Yes, I did,' said Daphne. 'That's why I picked up. And yes, it is. Apart from anything else, I don't think you could get that desk out of the room without taking it apart.'

'Wonderful,' said Pippa. 'Daphne, could you do something for me? Could you look out of the window in that room, and tell me if you can see a willow tree?'

There was a silence, which lengthened. Finally Daphne spoke. 'A willow tree, dear?'

'It might have been cut down,' said Briony. 'Still searching.'

'I know it's an odd request,' said Pippa. 'But we think we've found a clue in Clementina's last poem.'

'Hold on a moment,' said Daphne. 'I'll have to put the phone down when I go upstairs.'

Pippa heard a clunk, then a gentle sigh. 'This is so weird,' said Pippa.

'Tell me about it,' said Briony. 'I didn't think I'd be playing hunt the willow. Oh, hang on a minute. Here we go.' She smoothed the page, and read.

'*The willow outside my window is so pretty, and yet so sad. It makes me think of weeping maidens, trailing their long hair and drooping like dying flowers. Sometimes I think I should tell Charles to get it cut down. But on other days I forget the maidens, and see only the fresh green leaves.*'

'I bet she did,' said Pippa, grimly. 'I hope Charles didn't cut it down.' She winced as loud clattering assaulted her ear.

'Hello?' gasped Daphne. 'Are you still there?'

'We're still here,' said Pippa. She couldn't bring herself to ask.

'Yes,' said Daphne, 'there is a willow. It's right at the end of the garden and there are two other trees in front of it, so it's hard to see. But it's big, and it's old. It's always been there, as far as I remember.'

'Daphne,' said Pippa, 'might we come over? There's something we need to tell you, and if we're right about this tree—'

'Oh, did Clementina write about the tree?' said Daphne. She sounded rather pleased.

'In a manner of speaking,' said Pippa. 'Would it be all right if we brought someone with us? Someone official?'

'You're not going to bring that young policeman, are you?' said Daphne. 'He gives me the willies.'

'No, we won't be bringing PC Gannet,' said Pippa.

'Oh,' said Daphne. 'That's all right, then. So long as it isn't Jeremy Lightfoot.'

'It definitely won't be Jeremy Lightfoot,' said Pippa. 'Briony and I will get to you as soon as we can.'

'Who's your official?' said Briony, looking amused.

'I need to see if he's still talking to me first,' said Pippa. 'I'll text my mother-in-law and see if she can pick Freddie up for me.' She typed a message, pressed *Send*, then scrolled through her contacts and put the phone to her ear.

'I know I messed up last time,' she said, as soon as the call connected, 'but I think you'll find this interesting.'

'Mmm,' said Jim. 'After last time, Pippa, you'll have to sell it better than that. Especially as I'm on a day off.' But he didn't sound cross.

'OK,' said Pippa. 'Imagine a cold case. The coldest case you ever saw. In fact, so cold that no one even knew it was a case. And the only clue is a poem that no one has ever been able to make sense of. Until now…'

'What have you been reading, Pippa?' said Jim. 'Is this to do with that poet you were going on about?'

'Are you interested, or not?' said Pippa.

'I didn't say I wasn't interested,' said Jim. 'And since I'm not at work, this doesn't count as official police business and I won't get carpeted.'

'In that case,' said Pippa, 'I'll see you at Daphne Fairhurst's house as soon as you can get there. And if you could bring a spade and any other garden tools you have, we'd be much obliged.'

'Digging for victory, eh?' said Jim.

'You could say that,' said Pippa.

Chapter 24

'I suppose Jeremy Lightfoot is coming,' said Marge.

'Of course he's coming,' said Pippa. 'He can't wait to get his paws on those letters.'

'He's got a funny way of showing it,' grumbled Marge. 'Didn't you say seven o'clock? It's a quarter past now.'

Pippa looked around the table. As she had often seen in gatherings, the people attending had taken the same seats as they had occupied the previous time. Daphne and Marge were together, with Pippa next to Marge, Malcolm and Norm sat opposite, and Lady Higginbotham was at the bottom of the horseshoe. The only noticeable difference was that they had been joined by Briony, who sat on Pippa's other side, chewing a nail.

It was twenty past seven when the door of the church hall creaked open and Jeremy Lightfoot swept in. 'I'm so sorry I'm late,' he said, 'I had trouble getting a taxi from the station.' He advanced to the table placed in the centre of the horseshoe, and set down his laptop bag. 'It's lovely to see you all again. As well as discussing what to do about the letters, it's the perfect opportunity to update you on plans for the literary festival.' He gazed around the room with a smug smile on his face, which dissolved when his eyes fell on Briony. 'Who is this?' he asked, glancing at Pippa. 'We agreed we would keep this meeting to the original participants. I don't think bringing your assistant is really in the spirit of that.'

Pippa glanced at Briony, who appeared to be having difficulty in speaking. 'Jeremy, may I introduce Dr Briony Shepherd. I've been helping her with a few things, and I felt it would be only right for her to attend the meeting.'

'What sort of things?' Jeremy asked. 'Have you been making more unfounded accusations? Because if you have —'

'Why don't we get on to the purpose of the meeting,' said Pippa. 'I believe you wanted to discuss the letters.'

Jeremy Lightfoot appeared a little less ruffled. 'Yes, indeed.' He sat behind the small table, looking like a teacher surveying his class. 'Now that the letters have been returned, it is time to determine their future destiny. Of course they should never have gone astray in the first place, but let's not think of that. Let's consider how the letters can be safeguarded and preserved for future generations.' He turned to Daphne. 'Daphne, it must have been a terrible ordeal for you, not knowing where the letters were, and worrying over losing an important part of your family's heritage—'

'It was certainly rather trying,' said Daphne. 'But I must admit that I haven't decided what to do yet.'

'Do you need more time?' asked Jeremy,

sympathetically.

'It isn't that,' said Daphne. 'It's more that some interesting new information has come to light.'

'New information?' said Jeremy. 'What sort of new information?' He looked around the group. 'Why has no one informed me of this?'

'Well, Jeremy,' said Pippa, 'when you contacted Daphne about the letters and I invited you to this meeting, you did say you were busy with your other work, so there hasn't been an opportunity to tell you—'

'Tell me what?' snapped Jeremy.

'I'll tell you now,' said Pippa. 'If you swap places with me.'

Jeremy studied her for a long moment, not bothering to disguise his contempt. 'Very well,' he said, getting up and strolling around the horseshoe to her place. 'Let's hear this new information.'

Pippa and Briony advanced to the small table, and Pippa put Jeremy Lightfoot's bag on the floor. Jeremy Lightfoot tutted, but said nothing.

'It's been an interesting few weeks,' said Pippa. 'Having read some Victorian poetry at school, I never thought I'd read any more. But as it turns out, I have. The occasion, of course, was the first of these meetings. But I really became interested in the poems when the letters went missing. Given that most of the poems were so dull, who on earth would want to steal the letters? Daphne asked me to investigate privately, rather than involve the police in the matter, and I admit that I jumped to the wrong conclusion. You, Jeremy, were the obvious suspect, but as we now know, that was not the case.'

'Indeed,' said Jeremy. 'Not your finest hour.'

'No, it wasn't,' said Pippa, 'and I'm sorry. But by this point I was caught up in a different mystery. I wanted to understand what was so interesting about Clementina Stoate that someone would take the letters. I approached Briony, who is a specialist in Victorian literature, to see if she could shed any light on the problem, and Daphne kindly loaned us the only remaining volume of Clementina's journal.'

'Her journal?' said Jeremy, half getting up from his seat. 'What journal? There is no journal.'

'Oh, but there is,' said Briony. 'And it's incredibly interesting, both for what it does say, and what it doesn't. You see, no one has ever really understood Clementina Stoate's late creative flowering and her subsequent retirement from poetry altogether. In her journal Clementina talked a little of her maid, Mary, with whom she was very frustrated. If you remember, Jeremy, you read us a letter of Clementina's which mentioned her.'

Jeremy rolled his eyes. 'Have I really come all this way to listen to some junior lecturer raving about a maid?'

'I'm afraid so,' said Briony. 'At first we thought Clementina's newfound creativity was stimulated by her conflict with Mary. But the more we read, the more suspicious we grew. Mary was wilful, rebellious. She liked to take walks, and as you know most of Clementina's best poems are about nature. Clementina enjoyed punishing her and getting her under control, and there was an interesting incident where she sneaked into the servants' bedrooms, gathered up all Mary's papers, and apparently burnt them. But we don't think she did. We think that Mary wrote those poems, and Clementina stole them.'

'This is absolutely ridiculous,' said Jeremy. 'You're just embarrassing yourself.'

'Am I?' said Briony, opening her eyes wide. 'Perhaps, then, I'd better not share our interpretation of Clementina's last poem, "The Key". Reading it in the light of what we now surmised, we managed to crack it. No one has ever been sure what the poem meant. However, with a bit of rooting in cold, hard fact, provided by Pippa, we did some digging. Actual digging. And we'd like to show you the result.'

Briony turned her head, and called towards the kitchen. 'Could you bring it in, please?'

The first person they saw was Jim Horsley, in uniform, holding the door open for a tall, thin man in a tweed jacket and a maroon bow tie, carrying a largish metal box swaddled in a white cloth as though it were a crown on a cushion. 'May I introduce Constable Horsley and Dr Martin Paisley, the head of Gadcestershire Archives.'

Dr Paisley didn't acknowledge the introduction, but walked steadily to the table, and set the box down. 'We are still working on it,' he said. 'So far, though, everything checks out. The box is Victorian, the paper is of a make known at the time, and the ink is also consistent with what I would expect. Even at this stage, I would be prepared to vouch that this box is genuine.'

'And I was there when it was dug up from Miss Fairhurst's back garden,' said Jim Horsley. 'The ground was completely undisturbed, and clearly had been for some time.'

'We found the box buried beneath the roots of an old willow tree which was visible from Clementina's window,' said Pippa. 'The window has an oak frame. I'm sure you remember the opening of "The Key", Jeremy.'

Jeremy looked utterly disgusted, as if Clementina had tricked him by making the puzzle so easy. 'So what's inside?' he asked, leaning forward in spite of himself.

'I was hoping you'd ask that,' said Briony. 'Martin, would you be able to open the box and perhaps show us a couple of items?'

'Of course.' Martin Paisley took a pair of gloves from his pocket, and put them on. 'The box was locked, of course,' he said. 'However, when Pippa and Briony brought it to me we were able to find a key that fitted, since it is a box of fairly common make.' He opened the box, drew out a piece of paper in a protective cover, and laid it on the table. 'This paper shows a manuscript version of "Daisies at Dawn", here simply called "Daisies". You will observe that the handwriting is very different from that of Clementina Stoate's letters, which Pippa and Briony brought along for comparison. This hand is round and, dare I say it, childish, and the manuscript contains many crossings-out and amendments. It is not signed, but further evidence from the box suggests extremely strongly that this is the work of Mary Wright.'

'She could have copied it out,' said Jeremy, spreading his hands. 'She could have been making trouble.'

'The further evidence which Martin refers to,' said

Briony, 'is Clementina's journal. Her real one. Pippa and I had both observed that when Clementina became famous, her journal entries were shorter and less frequent.'

Martin opened the box again, removed his gloves, and took out a black notebook, smaller than the journal Daphne had given to Pippa, and with a brass lock on the front. 'This,' said Briony, 'is the reason why. Martin, could you read us the bookmarked entries, please?'

'I can't say it would be a pleasure,' said Martin, 'but yes, I shall.' He opened the journal where a slip of paper had been inserted, and began to read.

20th July 1878

She knows. I know it. I found my copy of Chapman's Magazine, the one containing the poems, in the drawing room this morning. It was not where I had left it, and the pages were crumpled. And when she waited on us at dinner, I caught her looking at me, and the expression on her face—

I don't know what to do. I am tempted to invent a missing piece of jewellery, and turn her away without a character. But what if she tells someone? What if she writes to Mr Chapman?

He might not believe her. How could a common housemaid write a poem like that? But I cannot take the risk. I must decide what to do; but my brain jumps from possibility to possibility, and settles on nothing.

Martin cleared his throat. 'The next entry is the day after.'

I lay awake all night tossing and turning, but I have had an idea. I shall send Abigail out on an errand, and I shall speak to Mary, and invite her to talk with me. Not in the house, for there is too much risk of overhearing. Somewhere outside. Yes, that will do.

Martin looked up. 'I shall move on two days.'

23 July 1878
It is done – it is over. I can sleep easy again.
I saw the triumph in her eyes this morning, when I asked her to take a walk with me later, but I was determined not to indulge it. 'Do not tell the others,' I said, 'for they will be jealous of you.'
She eyed me in that sly way she has. 'And will they have reason to be?' she said. 'I'm giving up some of my half-day.'
'Perhaps,' I said. 'You must wait until this evening, and see.'
I had told Mary to meet me in the meadow by the river at nine o'clock. I made a pretence to Charles that I was calling on a friend of mine who had asked me to bring her a book, and he accepted it without curiosity. Sometimes I wish he was more curious about my movements.
Mary was a full ten minutes late. I could see the insolent gleam in her eye, and the pleasure that she took in keeping me waiting. Her first words to me were 'I know what you did.'
I drew myself up to my full height. 'And what did I do, pray?'

'You stole my poems. I looked at that magazine you left out, and I saw them. You changed the titles, but I'm not stupid. You said you burnt my papers, and you never did. You took them for yourself!'

'And what will you do about it?' I asked. 'Who will believe you, a semi-literate maid?'

'I'll make them believe,' she said. 'I'll write more, and I'll send them to your Mr Chapman, and see what he thinks.'

'You will not,' I said. 'Not under my roof. Consider yourself dismissed. Go back to the house, and pack your box immediately.'

'Can you really afford to dismiss me?' said Mary. 'Don't you think it would be better to keep me on, and give me a raise? In fact, you should give all of us servants a raise. You pay starvation wages.'

'You ungrateful wretch!' Anger consumed me. I seized hold of her wrist and marched her to the river. It was dark now, and no one could see us. I twisted her arm behind her back and made her kneel on the riverbank, and put her head under the water. 'How dare you insult my charity!' I counted to twenty before I let her up for air. 'Apologise,' I said.

'You're a bitch and a thief!' she cried, and I ducked her again. This time I counted to forty, and I could feel her struggles lessening. I dragged her out by the scruff of the neck and put my mouth to her ear. 'Apologise,' I said.

'I'm going to write to the newspapers about you!' she shouted. 'You'll be thrown in prison for your cruelty and your thieving ways!'

So I put her head into the water, and this time I held her until she struggled no more. Then I pushed her limp body into the river.

Martin looked at Daphne, who was weeping quietly. 'I'm sorry,' he said.

'It's all right,' said Daphne. 'I have read it myself, and it needs to be heard. But it's horrible.'

'It is,' said Briony. 'We now know from the contents of this box that Mary wrote many poems, and Clementina chose a selection to present as her own work. In all, there are around a hundred poems written by Mary Wright in existence.' She glanced at Daphne. 'May we read the last extract?'

Daphne nodded. 'You may as well,' she said. 'It's not as bad as the last one. I mean it is, but—' She subsided into quiet, hiding behind her handkerchief.

Martin cleared his throat in an embarrassed manner, turned to the end of the journal, and read.

22nd November 1890

It has been a strange life, this. It is not over, and yet it is, for I can publish no more poetry. Mary is silent, and now Charles is silent too, and my desire to be known, and to be well thought of, has brought it about. This will be my last entry. I have no wish to pursue fame and fortune any more. I only wish to live a quiet, contemplative life, however much of it is left.

I ought to burn Mary's poems. Perhaps I should have burnt them when I found them, and yet what good would that have done? I have enjoyed success in a way that she never could. Who would have believed her? It is for the best that I performed the role of an editor, suppressing the unwiser outpourings of an immature mind, and giving a much-needed polish to the rough gems which I uncovered.

At any rate, it is over. Poor Pipit has died; he chirped his last this morning. I have asked William the valet to dig a hole beneath the willow tree, to bury him. But the box I shall bury will contain this journal and Mary's papers. And that will be the end of it.

Martin closed the book, and bowed his head.

'We'll never know why Clementina wrote and published "The Key",' said Pippa. 'Perhaps out of guilt, so that if anyone could solve the mystery they would find out what really happened. Or perhaps she was inspired one last precious time, and couldn't bear to waste the opportunity.'

Everyone was silent for some time. Jeremy Lightfoot was the first to break it. 'So what happens now?' he asked. 'Who owns these poems?'

'Not me,' said Daphne. 'They are absolutely nothing to do with me, and I couldn't be happier.' Her face lit up with an almost fierce glee. 'I have lived under the shadow of that woman my whole life, and how I regret it.'

'But who does own them?' Jeremy persisted. 'This Mary was unmarried, and had no children—'

'And that's why we asked Gadcestershire Archives, along with Malcolm here, to do a little investigating,' said Pippa.

Malcolm cleared his throat, and everyone turned to

look at him. 'I took the liberty of drawing up a small family tree,' he said, unrolling a long piece of paper. 'Mary had a younger sister, Martha, who married and had six children. The oldest of those was Mary, born in 1886. She married a man called John Kerslake, and they had four children. The oldest child, also Mary, was born in 1914, and married a man called William Apsley. And their oldest child is Margaret Margison, née Apsley' – he smiled shyly – 'whom we know as Marge, born in 1944.'

'How convenient,' said Jeremy, sourly.

Marge beamed. 'It is, rather,' she said. 'It keeps everything in the village. And by great fortune my niece just happens to be a Victorian specialist. So I shall let Briony decide what is best to do, and I am confident that she will make wise decisions.'

Jeremy snorted. 'Well, there certainly won't be any literary festival now. Not with all this scandal.'

'Oh, I don't know,' said Briony. 'I've had quite a busy week. I had a chat with someone at the Arts Council, and they were very interested in funding a potential event this summer. Oh yes, and the University of Gadcestershire Press have already approved my book proposal for the *Collected Poems of Mary Wright*.'

'Go on, tell him about the other book,' said Pippa.

'Do you think I should?' Briony asked Pippa.

Pippa grinned. 'Oh yes.'

'Very well,' said Briony, smiling back. 'Pippa's friend Serendipity has a literary agent, to whom I sent another book proposal, and he says he's getting a lot of interest. It will tell the story of how Pippa and I uncovered the truth about Clementina Stoate, interspersed with extracts from Clementina's journal and a study of female agency in the Victorian period. He thinks it might even go to a publishers' auction.'

'Congratulations,' said Jeremy Lightfoot, and his voice was as dry as a bone. 'I'll leave you all to your celebrations, since I'm clearly not needed here.'

'Oh, but you are needed, Jeremy,' said Pippa. 'I'm sure the production company will want you to appear.'

'The production company?' said Jeremy, turning his head this way and that like a hound on the scent.

'Yes,' said Pippa. 'Serendipity's manager knows someone who works in television, and they've commissioned a documentary for the autumn schedules. I'm sure the company would love to interview you, and get the, um, traditional academic angle.'

Jeremy Lightfoot sprang out of his chair, stalked towards the door, spoiled his exit completely by going back for his laptop bag, and left without another word.

'Well, he wanted a meeting,' said Daphne. 'And I think we gave him one.'

'That we did,' said Marge, and chuckled. 'That was most enjoyable. Better than TV.'

'But was it better than Fortnite?' asked Pippa, with a smile.

Marge considered. 'Comparable,' she said, nodding. 'Different, but comparable.'

'If we're finished,' said Martin, 'I'll get this box packed up and safely in the archives.' He paused, and looked around him. 'How odd to be back in this village so soon.'

'Oh, were you here recently, then?' asked Pippa.

'For a flying visit, yes,' said Martin. 'I had dinner and stayed over with a friend in Gadding Parva, and I was passing through the next morning when I remembered that someone I'd met at a party mentioned a wonderful stained-glass dragon in the church at Much Gadding. Paula, I think her name was.'

'What, the dragon?' said Marge.

'No, no, the person,' said Martin. 'But it turned out to be the wrong church, and there was no dragon anyway. So I drove off to work.'

'Another mystery solved,' murmured Pippa.

'Excuse me?' said Briony.

Pippa laughed. 'Don't mind me,' she said. 'There is mystery everywhere, if you can only find it.'

Chapter 25

'And do you think people will be interested in these new poems that you have discovered, Dr Shepherd?' asked Caroline Denny, chief reporter on *Gadcestershire Today*, waving a hand at Daphne's house.

Briony considered, but not for too long. 'I certainly hope so,' she said. 'It's very unusual to find such a complete body of unknown work. I also hope it will encourage people to take a fresh look at the poems which we thought had been written by Clementina Stoate. Now we know they were written by a young housemaid, rather than a comparatively established poet, that may change the way we read them.'

'How interesting,' said Caroline. 'Pippa, when you first picked up a copy of Clementina's poems at the library, did you ever think you would become embroiled in yet another case?'

Pippa paused for a moment, diverted by a struggle on the village green between Lila and Ruby. 'I had absolutely no idea,' she said. 'I thought I might help to organise a small event, and instead it became something completely different.'

'And there you have it,' said Caroline Denny. 'It began as a series of charming nature poems, and it ended with a poet turned murderer. Caroline Denny, *Gadcestershire Today*.'

'And cut,' said the cameraman, who was also directing. 'Take a break, everyone.'

Caroline smiled politely at Pippa and Briony, then wandered across the road towards the camera. 'Could I watch it back?'

'You can, but I'm not shooting it again,' the cameraman replied. 'That was the third take, and we need to be out of here soon if I'm going to get this edited for the early-evening news.'

'I ought to head off,' said Briony, with a look of regret. 'My nine am class on *Middlemarch* will seem tame after this.'

Pippa laughed. 'I imagine it will,' she said. 'But hopefully this will open doors.'

'Hopefully. The head of department has asked if I can pop in and see him tomorrow. I'm hoping it isn't even more marking. And if he's in a really good mood, I'll ask if I can free up a day a week to work on this.'

'Fingers crossed,' said Pippa. 'Excuse me a moment, Briony, my daughter is trying to escape.' She crossed the road and hurried across the green to where Ruby had wriggled free and was chasing a duck. 'Ruby, please leave the ducks alone,' she said. 'Sorry, Lila.'

'It's all right,' said Lila, who looked distinctly green.

Pippa studied her. 'I thought morning sickness was meant to happen in the morning?'

'Theoretically, yes,' said Lila, reaching into her pocket for a boiled sweet. 'I was just the same with Bella. Remind me why I thought having another kid was a good idea, will you?'

'Hormones,' said Pippa.

'Keep your voice down,' hissed Lila. 'No one's supposed to know.'

'Mmm,' said Pippa. 'I think they may guess.' She grinned. 'How is Jeff taking it?'

Lila managed a slightly wobbly smile. 'He's over the moon,' she said. 'As it turns out, he really wanted to talk about having kids, but he was scared to bring it up in case I felt that he was pressuring me, or that I was too old... Not that I am too old, obviously, but—'

'Of course not,' said Pippa. 'And I'm sorry to saddle you with Ruby, but I knew Sheila would be as much use as a chocolate teapot.'

Sheila had wandered over to the OB van and buttonholed the person inside. Then she turned, surveyed the scene, and pointed in Pippa's direction.

'Oh God, she's saying that she knows me,' said Pippa. 'Hopefully that means she's forgiven me. She was extremely cross when she found out that I'd sent her to pick up Freddie because I was helping to dig up murder evidence from Daphne's back garden.'

The cameraman waved his arms for attention. 'Caroline, could you redo that segment with the policeman...? I've checked it and you're in a kind of weird shadow.'

Jim Horsley unpeeled himself from the tree he was leaning against and sauntered towards Daphne's house. Pippa couldn't tell whether he was enjoying the experience or embarrassed by it, for his face was shadowed by the peak of his cap.

'Would you mind taking off your hat?' called the cameraman, as Caroline walked over to Jim.

Jim obliged, dropped the hat behind Daphne's front wall, and ran his fingers through his hair to tidy it. *He's enjoying it*, thought Pippa. *Poor PC Gannet. A murder investigation right under his nose, and he still managed to miss it.*

Sheila, presumably sent on her way, came to join them. 'I never realised there was so much to television,' she said. 'Is someone watching out for Ruby?'

'She's there,' said Pippa, pointing to where Ruby was sitting cross-legged on the grass, picking daisies. 'I don't think even Ruby can get into too much trouble.'

'Oh yes, how is Cygnets going?' asked Lila. 'I can't believe I'm going through this again. I must be mad.'

'You'll be fine,' said Pippa. 'It's just the nausea talking.'

'And the lack of sleep,' said Lila. 'I'd forgotten about that, too.' Then she grinned. 'At least this time I know what I'm in for.'

'Won't Freddie be cross that he's missed this?' said Sheila. 'And it's a shame that Simon couldn't take time off work.'

'He can watch it later,' said Pippa. 'On the news.'

***

Simon arrived home bang on time, bearing a bottle of wine and a box of chocolates. 'Good heavens,' said Pippa, taking the wine from him and inspecting the label. 'I must get myself on TV more often.'

'We'll see,' said Simon. 'If it's too embarrassing, I may have to drink it all myself.' Then he leaned in and kissed her. 'Not really,' he murmured in her ear. 'I'm sure it will be great, and I'm very proud of you.'

'It was a joint effort,' said Pippa. 'Briony did at least as much as I did. And if Daphne hadn't let us borrow the journal, none of this would ever have come to light.'

'How is Daphne?' asked Simon. 'Was she at the filming?'

'No,' said Pippa. 'They asked her, but she said she'd rather not be interviewed. She rang me up and told me. She isn't upset; it's more that she wants to have a quiet life. In fact, she told me she's going to contact the National Trust and see if they would like to take the house on. If not, she's planning to sell it.'

Simon grinned. 'Maybe she could swap with Marge,' he said. 'Do you know what she's planning to do?'

Pippa shrugged. 'I think she'll be guided by Briony,' she said. 'Marge won't be beaten down by Mary's legacy in the way that Daphne was by Clementina's. She's too sensible.'

'And too bolshy,' said Simon.

'That too,' said Pippa. 'Anyway, let's get this wine in the fridge and sort the kids out. We have an important television programme to watch.'

In the end, their segment of *Gadcestershire Today* lasted a good ten minutes. It included Pippa and Briony's interview, the interview with Jim, a small clip with Martin Paisley at the archives, and a voice-over from Caroline. Jeremy Lightfoot was noticeable by his absence, though he was mentioned in passing. 'All in all,' said Caroline to camera, 'an amazing story of literary detection where two modern women uncovered the troubled relationship of two very different Victorians. Caroline Denny, *Gadcestershire Today*.'

Simon worked his right arm out from behind Pippa and applauded, then gave her a gentle squeeze. 'That was brilliant,' he said. 'And you were ace.'

'Was I?' said Pippa. 'Could you tell that Ruby was distracting me?'

'Not really,' said Simon. 'You had a bit of a faraway look in your eyes, but most people would assume you were thinking about the past.'

'Instead of wondering whether Ruby was going to escape and run into the duck pond,' said Pippa. 'I'll take that.' She paused. 'I thought everyone did well.'

'They did,' said Simon. 'I thought your Briony might be a bit scary, but actually she was great. Informative but accessible.'

'Maybe she'll give Jeremy Lightfoot a run for his money,' said Pippa.

'Maybe,' said Simon. 'I was surprised they interviewed Jim Horsley. He only came in at the end, when you rang him up.' He frowned. 'Why did you phone him? Doesn't he work in Gadcester now?'

'Nothing to do with me,' said Pippa. 'Daphne doesn't like PC Gannet, so I didn't have a choice.'

Simon shrugged. 'Fair enough.' Then he pointed at the television. 'Are you recording this?' A smile spread over his face.

'Of course I'm recording this,' said Pippa. 'When the kids are older I can show them the time when Mummy was on TV.'

'Bless,' said Simon. 'I'm sure this won't be the last time.'

'Well, no,' said Pippa. 'I mean, there's that documentary.'

'Oh, I know,' said Simon. 'But I don't think that will be the last time either.' He kissed Pippa on the cheek. 'You're a famous detective, Pippa Parker.'

'I wouldn't go that far,' said Pippa, feeling her cheeks warm up.

'A famous detective,' said Simon, 'and a modest one.'

Pippa stared at him. 'Have you started on the wine without me?'

'No chance,' said Simon. 'I don't want to be tracked down and apprehended by my own wife.'

'That won't ever happen,' said Pippa. 'So long as you pour me a glass too.'

'I'll drink to that,' said Simon. 'Back in a moment.' He kissed her again, and padded to the kitchen.

What a case, thought Pippa. *What a ridiculous, frustrating, exasperating, fascinating case. And it isn't over yet. There are Mary's poems to read, and Clementina's secret journal, and trying to uncover whether she did murder Charles...* She shivered, and snuggled further into the sofa. *But that's for another day. For now, we've solved the case, and I'm happy.* And she smiled at Simon as he entered the sitting room and handed her a glass of wine.

Acknowledgements

As ever, my first thanks go to my beta readers – Carol Bissett, Ruth Cunliffe, Paula Harmon, and Stephen Lenhardt – and to my meticulous proofreader, John Croall. I left that typo in for you specially! Thank you all for your input; it does make a huge difference.

The idea for this book came, I think, at least partly from two other books I've read fairly recently. The first is *Possession* by AS Byatt (that was a re-read and I found it as intriguing as I did the first time round). The second is *The Daughter of Time* by Josephine Tey. If you haven't read either, I'd recommend them!

Again, a big thank you to my husband Stephen, who put up with me pacing around our small back garden (lockdown restrictions, you see) with his characteristic good humour. Even that time when I didn't see him because I was busy in the nineteenth century, and I let out a very cross yelp.

But my final thanks go to you, the reader. I hope you've enjoyed Pippa's latest mystery, and if you have, a short review on Amazon or Goodreads would be very much appreciated. Ratings and reviews, however short, help readers to discover books.

FONT AND IMAGE CREDITS

Fonts:

Brisbane by Larin Type Co.

Chemy Retro, licensed via The Hungry JPEG.

Dancing Script OT by Impallari Type: www.fontsquirrel.com/fonts/dancing-script-ot. SIL Open Font License v.1.10: http://scripts.sil.org/OFL.

Edo Regular by Vic Fieger (freeware): www.fontsquirrel.com/fonts/Edo.

Nimbus Roman No 9L by URW++: https://www.fontsquirrel.com/fonts/nimbus-roman-no9-l. GNU General Public License v2.00: https://www.fontsquirrel.com/license/nimbus-roman-no9-l.

Gibsons Co by Design and co.

Buffalo by HanzelStudio.

Graphics:

Magnifying glass: CMYK Fingerprints free vector by freepik: https://www.freepik.com/free-vector/cmyk-fingerprints_759311.htm.

Pens: Set of realistic literature objects by macrovector: https://www.freepik.com/free-vector/set-realistic-literature-objects-pens-with-inkwell-vintage-books-typewriter-isolated_6804346.htm.

Cover created using GIMP image editor: www.gimp.org.

About the Author

Liz Hedgecock grew up in London, England, did an English degree, and then took forever to start writing. After several years working in the National Health Service, some short stories crept into the world. A few even won prizes. Then the stories started to grow longer…

Now Liz travels between the nineteenth and twenty-first centuries, murdering people. To be fair, she does usually clean up after herself.

Liz's reimaginings of Sherlock Holmes, her Pippa Parker cozy mystery series, the Caster & Fleet Victorian mystery series (written with Paula Harmon), the Magical Bookshop series, and the Maisie Frobisher Mysteries are available in ebook and paperback.

Liz lives in Cheshire with her husband and two sons, and when she's not writing or child-wrangling you can usually find her reading, messing about on Twitter, or cooing over stuff in museums and art galleries. That's her story, anyway, and she's sticking to it.

Website/blog: http://lizhedgecock.wordpress.com
Facebook: http://www.facebook.com/lizhedgecockwrites
Twitter: http://twitter.com/lizhedgecock
Goodreads: https://www.goodreads.com/lizhedgecock
Amazon author page: http://author.to/LizH

Books by Liz Hedgecock

Pippa Parker Mysteries (novels)
Murder At The Playgroup
Murder In The Choir
A Fete Worse Than Death
Murder in the Meadow
The QWERTY Murders
Past Tense

The Magical Bookshop (novels)
Every Trick in the Book
Brought to Book
Double Booked
By the Book
Black Books
Fully Booked

Caster & Fleet Mysteries (with Paula Harmon)
The Case of the Black Tulips
The Case of the Runaway Client
The Case of the Deceased Clerk
The Case of the Masquerade Mob
The Case of the Fateful Legacy
The Case of the Crystal Kisses

Maisie Frobisher Mysteries (novels)
All At Sea
Off The Map
Gone To Ground
In Plain Sight

Mrs Hudson & Sherlock Holmes series (novels)
A House Of Mirrors
In Sherlock's Shadow
A Spider's Web

Sherlock & Jack series (novellas)
A Jar Of Thursday
Something Blue
A Phoenix Rises

Halloween Sherlock series (novelettes)
The Case of the Snow-White Lady
Sherlock Holmes and the Deathly Fog
The Case of the Curious Cabinet

Short stories
The Secret Notebook of Sherlock Holmes
Bitesize
The Adventure of the Scarlet Rosebud
The Case of the Peculiar Pantomime (a Caster & Fleet short mystery)
Christmas Presence

For children (with Zoe Harmon)
A Christmas Carrot

Printed in Great Britain
by Amazon